Mia Couto wa[...]
Beira. In the [...]
medical studies but [...]
ment in the independence struggle and the start of a career in
journalism. He was to become director of the Mozambique
Information Agency (AIM), and the magazine *Tempo* and later
the official daily newspaper *Notícias*.

His poems have appeared in Mozambican magazines since
he was 14 and in 1983 his first volume of poetry *Raiz de orvalho*
(Root of Dew) was published. *Vozes Anoitecidas*, now translated
as *Voices Made Night*, was first published in Mozambique in
1986, meriting a second edition there the following year.
Subsequently it was published in Portugal and Italy, where it
gained wide critical acclaim. The stories have also been
adapted for radio and stage.

Mia Couto lives and works in Maputo as a journalist and
has also taken up university studies once more. In 1988 he
was awarded a prize by the Organisation of Mozambican
Journalists (ONJ) for his regular 'cronicando' columns in
Notícias, which the newspaper published in book form in 1989.

David Brookshaw has a PhD in Brazilian literature from
the University of London. Since 1978, he has been
Lecturer in Portuguese in the Department of Hispanic, Portu-
guese and Latin American Studies at the University of Bristol.
He has a specialist interest in literature and national identity.
He is the author of *Race and Color in Brazilian Literature*, and
Paradise Betrayed: Brazilian Literature of the Indian, and has also
published articles on African literature in Portuguese.

MIA COUTO

VOICES MADE NIGHT

Translated by David Brookshaw

HEINEMANN

Heinemann International
a division of Heinemann Educational Books Ltd
Halley Court, Jordan Hill, Oxford OX2 8EJ

Heinemann Educational Books Inc
70 Court Street, Portsmouth, New Hampshire, 03801, USA

Heinemann Educational Books (Nigeria) Ltd
PMB 5205, Ibadan
Heinemann Kenya Ltd
PO Box 45314, Nairobi, Kenya
Heinemann Educational Boleswa
PO Box, 10103, Village Post Office, Gaborone, Botswana
Heinemann Educational Books (Caribbean) Ltd
175 Mountain View Avenue, Kingston 6, Jamaica

LONDON   EDINBURGH   MELBOURNE   SYDNEY
AUCKLAND   SINGAPORE   MADRID
ATHENS   BOLOGNA

British Library Cataloguing in Publication Data

Couto, Mia
Voices made night – (African Writers Series)
1. Short stories in Portuguese. Mozambican writers, 1945–
– English texts
I. Title   II. Series   III. Vozes anoitecidas. *English*
869.3 [F]

ISBN 0–435–90570–8

Frontispiece illustrated by Paula Cox

Photoset by Wilmaset, Birkenhead, Wirral
Printed in Great Britain by
Cox and Wyman Ltd, Reading

90 91 92 93 94 10 9 8 7 6 5 4 3 2 1

CONTENTS

The most harrowing thing about poverty is the ignorance it has of itself. Faced by an absence of everything, men abstain from dreams, depriving themselves of the desire to be others. There exists in nothingness that illusion of plenitude which causes life to stop and voices to become night.

These stories always stirred in me as a result of something which had really happened but which had been told to me as though it had occurred on some distant shore of the world. While crossing that frontier of shadow, I listened to voices that drained the sun. Others were wings which bore my writing aloft in its flight. To both I dedicate this desire to relate and to invent.

The Fire

The old woman was seated on the mat, waiting motionless for her man to return from the bush. Her legs suffered a double weariness: from the time-worn by-ways, and from the times trodden.

Her worldly goods were spread out on the ground: bowls, baskets, a pestle. Around her was emptiness, even the wind was alone.

The old man approached slowly as was his custom. He had shepherded his sadness before him ever since his youngest sons had left on the road to no return.

'My husband is shrinking,' she thought. *'He is a shadow.'*

A shadow, yes indeed. But only of his soul, for he scarcely had any body left. The old man came nearer and draped his leanness on the neighbouring mat. He raised his head and, without looking at the woman, said:

'I'm thinking.'

'What is it you are thinking, husband?'

'If you die, how shall I, alone, sick and without strength, how shall I bury you?'

He passed his skinny fingers over the straw mat on which he was sitting, and went on:

'We are poor, all we have is nothingness. Nor do we have anybody else. I think it better that we start digging your grave now.'

The woman, touched, smiled:

'How good you are, my husband! I was lucky to have you as the man of my life.'

The old man fell silent, lost in thought. Only later did he open his mouth:

'I'm going to see if I can find a spade.'

'Where are you going to get a spade?'

'I'm going to see if they have one at the store.'

'Are you going all the way to the store? It is a long way.'

'I shall be back this side of night.'

All the silence remained hushed so that she might listen for her husband's return. When he came back, ragged tatters of dust were retaining the last rays of sun.

'Well then, husband?'

'It cost a lot of money,' and he held up the spade the better to show it to her. 'Tomorrow morning I'll start work on your grave.'

And they lay down on their separate mats. Softly, she interrupted his drift into sleep:

'But, husband . . .'

'What?'

'I'm not even ill.'

'You must be. You are so old.'

'Maybe,' she agreed. And they fell asleep.

The next morning he looked at her intensely.

'I'm measuring your size. After all, you're bigger than I thought.'

'Nonsense, I'm small.'

She went to the woodpile, and pulled out some faggots.

'The wood's almost finished, husband. I'll go to the bush to get some more.'

'Go, woman. I shall stay here and dig your graveyard.'

She was already moving away when an invisible hand seemed to tug at her *capulana** and, pausing, but still with her back to him, she said:

'Listen, husband. Let me ask one thing . . .'

*A dress worn by women, akin to a sarong.

'What is it you want?'

'Don't dig too deep. I want to be near the top, just below the ground, so that I'll almost be able to touch life a little.'

'Very well. I shan't put much earth on top of you.'

For two weeks the old man busied himself with the hole. The nearer he got to completing it, the longer he took. Then suddenly the rains came. The grave filled with water. It looked like a brazen little puddle. The old man cursed the clouds, and the heavens which had brought them.

'Don't talk silliness, you'll be punished for it,' she warned. More days of rain and the walls of the tomb began to cave in. The old man walked over and surveyed the damage. There and then he decided to go on. Soaked under a river of rain, the old man clambered in and out, his groans ever louder, the amount of soil he carried, ever less.

'Come on in out of the rain, husband. You can't keep on like this.'

'Stop fussing, woman,' ordered the old man. From time to time, he would pause to see how grey the sky was. He was trying to see who still had more work to do, himself or the rain.

On the following day, the old man was woken up by his own bones, which were pulling him further into his aching body.

'I'm in pain, woman. I can't get up.'

His wife turned to him and wiped the sweat from his face.

'You're full of fever. It's because of the soaking you got.'

'No it isn't, woman. It's because I slept near the fire.'

'What fire?'

His reply was a groan. The old woman got alarmed: what was this fire the man had seen if they hadn't even lit one?

She got up to take him his bowl of mealie porridge. When she turned round he was already up, looking for his spade. He grabbed it and crept out of the house. At every other step, he would pause to gather strength.

'Husband, don't go out like that. Eat first.'

He made some drunken gesture of dismissal. The old woman persisted:

3

'*You don't know your left from your right. Rest a little.*'

He was already inside the hole and getting ready to start work again. The fever punished him for his obstinacy, giddiness caused the sides of his world to dance before his eyes. Suddenly, he cried out in despair:

'*Woman, help me!*'

He fell like a severed branch, a cloud rent asunder. The old woman ran over to help him.

'*You're very sick.*'

Pulling him by the arms she brought him to the mat. He lay there taking deep breaths. All his life force was concentrated there, distributed among those ribs which rose and fell. In this lonely desert, you slide into death as quietly as a bird folding its wings. It does not come with a violent flash, such as happens in places where life glitters.

'*Woman,*' he said in a voice that left no trace, '*I can't leave you like this.*'

'*What is it you are thinking now?*'

'*I can't leave that grave without a use. I must kill you.*'

'*That is true, husband. You worked so hard to dig that hole. It is a pity that it should remain empty.*'

'*Yes, I'm going to have to kill you; but not today for I have no body for it.*'

She helped him to get up and made him a cup of tea.

'*Drink it, man. Drink to get better, for tomorrow you will need your strength.*'

The old man fell asleep, and the woman sat down in the doorway. In the shadow of her repose she watched the sun, king of light, gradually drain. She thought about the day and laughed to herself about its contradictions: she, whose birth had never been registered, now knew the date of her death. When the moon began to light up the trees in the wood, she leant back and fell asleep. She dreamed of times far away from there: her children were present, the dead ones and those still alive, the *machamba** was full of crops, her eyes slid over the green of it all. There was the old man in the middle, with his tie on, telling stories, lies for the most part. They were all there, her children and grandchildren. Life itself was there, unrolling, pregnant with promise. In that happy assembly, all believed in the truths of their elders, for they were always right, and no mother opened up her flesh to death. The noises of morning began to summon her out of herself, while she tried hard not to abandon her slumber. She begged night to stay so that her dream might linger, she begged this with the same devotion as when she had beseeched life not to take her children away.

She felt in the shadows for her husband's arm to give her strength in that moment of anguish. When she touched her companion's body with her hand, she saw that it was cold, so cold that it was as if, this time, he had fallen asleep far from that fire that no one had ever lit.

*Small plot of land for cultivation.

The Talking Raven's Last Warning

It happened right there, in the middle of the square, full of people queueing at the store. Zuzé Paraza, a retired painter, spat out bits of his two-a-penny cigarette. Then he coughed, shaking the gauntness of his body to its bones. Suddenly, so those who witnessed the event say, he vomited a live raven. The bird emerged whole from his belly. It had been so long inside him that it already knew how to talk. All covered in spittle, at first it didn't look like a bird. People gathered round Zuzé, peeping at the creature fallen from his cough. It shook itself free of its mucus covering, raised its beak, and to everyone's astonishment, uttered some words. With conviction, despite the bad pronunciation. Those present asked:

'*He's speaking, is he, the fellow?*'

Some laughed. But the voice of the women interrupted them:

'*Don't laugh.*'

Zuzé Paraza warned:

'*This is no ordinary bird. You'd better respect it.*'

'*Hey, Zuzé. Translate what he's saying for us. You must be able to understand the raven's dialect.*'

'*Of course I do. But not now, I don't want to translate now.*' And feeling himself the centre of attention, he added: '*This raven knows many secrets.*'

Then, placing the bird on his left shoulder, he withdrew, leaving behind him a babble of comments. So that was why the painter had those coughing fits. There was a stretch of sky

7

inside him. Or maybe it was the bird's feathers tickling his gullet. There were more questions than answers.

'Can a man give birth through his lungs?'

'Give birth to a bird? Not unless the old boy went around courting the she-ravens up there in the trees.'

'It's the soul of his dead wife that crossed over into the widower, you'll see.'

On the following day, Zuzé confirmed the latter version. The raven had come from the furthest frontier of life, nestled in his inside, and chosen a public moment for its apparition.

Others might take this opportunity to obtain information about their dear departed, the circumstances and whereabouts of their ancestors. Through the intermediary of the raven, they would be given answers to their questions. Requests came flocking in immediately. Zuzé no longer had a room, it was an office. He no longer talked to people but conducted a surgery. He gave special concessions, kept a long waiting list of appointments, and then made his clients wait. Payment was made according to a tariff: deceased within the current year, fifty escudos; communication with the deceased from the previous year, one hundred and fifty; those deceased outside the stated period, two hundred and fifty.

And this is where Dona Candida comes into the story, a mulatto woman of capacious virtue, a woman without enemies. Recently widowed, she was already an ex-widow. She married quickly second time round, to make up for the excesses of her abstinence. When she remarried, she chose Sulemane Amade, an Indian trader in the village. No time had gone by since her first husband, Evaristo Muchanga, had died.

But Candida could not keep herself to herself. Her body still yearned to be aroused, she was still of an age to be a mother. The truth is that in the interim she was never much of a widow. She was lonely by accident, not conviction. Her woman's needs never subsided.

'I got married. And so what? Do I need to explain?'

8

And with these words, Dona Candida began to tell of her complaint to Zuzé Paraza. When he knew he was being sought after, the fortune teller even brought forward the date of the consultation. He had never been visited by a mulatto woman. Zuzé's services had never been called upon from such a lofty quarter.

'I'm not just anyone, Senhor Paraza. How could such a thing happen to me?'

The buxom lady explained her troubles: her second marriage was proceeding without any mishaps. That is, until her new husband, Sulemane, began to suffer mysterious fits. They occurred at night, just when they were getting ready to make love. She would remove her bra; Sulemane's great bulk would turn towards her. It was then that the spell would have its effect: grunts instead of words, foam on the lips, eyes asquint.

'Sulemane,' she confessed, *'my own Sulemane jumps out of bed and then, still dressed, crawls on all fours, sniffs, rubs his belly on the floor and ends up snuffling the carpet. After that he's sweating so much that I have to give him water, and he knocks back one great big bottle. He doesn't return to his senses straightaway. He takes time to recover. He stutters, only hears on his right side, and goes to sleep with his eyes open. All night through those cross-eyes pretending they can see, it's horrible. Please, Senhor Zuzé, please help me. I'm going through such a hard time, and I'm even having my doubts about God. This is Evaristo's work, it's his curse. We were happy, Sulemane and I. Now the two of us are three. My God, why didn't I wait? Why doesn't he leave me alone?'*

Zuzé Paraza began to think while all the time stroking the raven. He had his suspicions: Evaristo was a black man, a native of the area. Dona Candida had probably not carried out all the rituals which would have freed her from her dead husband. He was wrong, she had.

'All the rituals?'

'Of course, Senhor Paraza.'

'But how? If you are brown in your skin and nearly white in your soul?'

9

'He was black, you know. It was his family who asked, and I obeyed.'
Paraza was intrigued, and still appeared to have his doubts.
'Did you kill the goat?'
'Yes, I did.'
'Did the animal bleat while you were singing?'
'It did.'
'And what else, Dona Candida?'
'I went to the river to wash his death off me. The widows took me and
bathed too. Then they took a piece of glass and cut me here, in the groin.
They told me it was there that my husband was sleeping. Poor things, if
they only knew where Evaristo was sleeping . . .'
'And did you bleed well?'
'Yes, all the blood came out. The widows saw it. From the blood they
said that I had come to an agreement with him. I didn't deny it. I thought
it better not to.'

Zuzé Paraza made a show of being deep in thought. Then, he
let the raven go. The creature fluttered about and alighted on
Candida's ample shoulder. She flinched, her flesh creeping
with ticklishness. She eyed the animal suspiciously. Seen from
that position, the raven was as ugly as can be. If you want to
admire the beauty of a bird, never look at its feet. The claws of a
bird preserve its scaly past, a legacy of creepy-crawling reptiles.

The raven turned this way and that on the mulatto woman's
smooth, round perch.

'Pardon me, Senhor Zuzé: he's not going to shit on top of me, is he?'
'Don't talk, Dona Candida. The creature needs to concentrate.'

Finally, the bird made its pronouncement. Zuzé listened
with his eyes closed, engaged in the effort of translation.

'What was it he said?'
'It wasn't the bird that spoke. It was Evaristo.'
'Evaristo?' she exclaimed doubtfully. 'With a voice like that?'
'Don't forget, he spoke through a beak.'

The fat woman became serious as she regained her confidence in him.

'Senhor Zuzé, now that you're on the line to him, ask him to . . .'

10

Changing her mind suddenly, Dona Candida ditched her medium, and began herself to shout at the raven perched on her shoulder:

'Evaristo, leave me in peace. Please leave me alone, and let me get on with my life quietly.'

The bird, upset by all the shouting, jumped from its perch. Paraza imposed some order:

'Dona Candida, it's no good getting flustered. You see? The bird got scared.'

His exhausted client began to sob.

'Did you listen to the dead man's request, Dona Candida?'

She shook her head. All she had heard was the raven, the same as all the other ravens that can be seen flitting around among the coconut palms.

'The deceased, Dona Candida, is asking for a suitcase full of clothes, the ones he used to wear.'

'But I haven't got his clothes any more. Didn't I tell you I carried out those rituals of yours? I ripped his clothes up, tore holes in them when he died. That's what they told me to do. They said I should make holes, that his clothes could let his last breath out. Yes, I know: if it happened now, I wouldn't cut anything up. I'd make use of everything. But at that time, Senhor Paraza . . .'

'This is very annoying, Dona Candida. The dead man really needs them. You just can't imagine the cold that the dead feel out there.'

The mulatto woman stood there, motionless, and imagined Evaristo shivering with cold, without a stitch of clothing to cover him. For all his wickedness, he didn't deserve such vengeance. She decided what to do: she would steal Sulemane's clothes and deliver them all in a concealed package.

'Sulemane mustn't know of this. My God, if he comes to suspect anything!'

'You can relax, Dona Candida. Nobody will know except for me and the raven.'

And as she was about to leave, the fat woman pondered:

'How is it that Evaristo, with all that jealousy he took with him to the

11

next world, how is it that he can agree to put on my new husband's clothes?'

'He will. Clothes are clothes. Cold is more powerful than jealousy.'

'Are you sure, Senhor Paraza?'

'That's my experience of the matter. The dead feel the cold because they are exposed to the wind and rain. That's why they envy the warmth of the living. You'll see, Dona Candida, these clothes will appease Evaristo and his desire for revenge.'

And the fat mulatto woman confessed her fear, which was neither totally of the dead, nor of the living:

'My fear now is of Sulemane. He will kill me, and you as well.'

Zuzé Paraza got to his feet confidently. He placed his hand on his client's arm and reassured her:

'I've been thinking to myself, Dona Candida, and I've found the answer. You will discover the robbery and tell your husband. There you are! It was some thief or other, there are so many round here.'

A week later, a suitcase arrived packed full of clothes. Trousers, shirts, underpants, ties, everything. A bonanza. Zuzé began by trying on the brown suit. It was large, cut to a trader's girth, a man used to being waited on, a man who ate well, whereas he, a painter, tended towards a slighter build. He was so skinny that neither bugs nor fleas chose him.

He rummaged around in the suitcase for a tie to match. There were more than ten, together with longjohns, and socks without holes. Sulemane must have been left without a pair of pants to his name. His clothes' cupboard must now be a nothing cupboard.

Dressed in the product of his deceit and inventiveness, Zuzé Paraza took out a bottle of *xicadju*. He knocked back more than ten glasses of the cashew liquor by way of celebration. It was then that the alcohol began to play tricks with his acuteness as well. A voice from deep inside kept telling him:

'These clothes are my own, no one gave them to me, and they came from nowhere. They're mine!'

And so, convinced he was the owner of such fineries, he

12

decided to go out and parade them. He stopped at the store, showed off his vanities, his jacket and tie. Voices around him were full of envy:

'Those clothes aren't his. I'm sure I've seen them on someone else.'

Racking their brains, those present finally arrived at the true owner: the clothes were Sulemane Amade's. Yes, of course, they were his. How had that bastard Zuzé got hold of them, that switchboard operator of the spirit world? The fellow had stolen them. That keeper of ravens had broken into Sulemane's house. And off they went to tell the Indian.

Unaware of such manoeuvres, Zuzé went on exhibiting his stolen goods. The raven observed him, cawing from above, while Zuzé, swaying and unswaying, played the role of chorus.

At this point, Sulemane arrived near the store, huffing and puffing with rage. He walked up to the painter and seized him by the scruff of the neck. Zuzé began to swing about in his oversize suit.

'How did you get hold of that suit, you thief?'

The painter tried to explain but was unable. The raven hopped around him, looking for a chance to perch on his limp head. When the Indian let up, Zuzé mumbled:

'Sulemane, don't kill me. I didn't steal these clothes. They were given to me.'

The Indian had not abandoned violence. He had merely changed his tactics: from throttling to kicking. Zuzé leapt about as if competing with the raven.

'Who gave you my clothes, you great crook?'

'Stop kicking me! I'll explain.'

Zuzé Paraza took advantage of a brief ceasefire, and came straight to the point.

'It was your wife, Sulemane. It was Dona Candida who gave me these clothes.'

'Candida gave them to you? That's a lie, you son-of-a-bitch.'

Blows, kicks, punches rained down on him while the bystanders cheered.

'*Tell the truth, Paraza. Don't shame me with stories about my wife.*'

But the old painter couldn't answer, for he was too busy trying to avoid the hiding he was getting. One of the punches flying in the direction of Paraza's nose hit the bird instead. Knocked flat, the raven spun round on the ground in its death throes, its wing broken. Everyone paused to watch the bird in its agony. Then, one or two anxious voices could be heard.

'*Sulemane, if you've killed the raven, then you'll be unlucky in your life.*'

'*Unlucky! Don't talk shit! Who is it that believes a raven can talk with spirits?*'

Zuzé, his nose bleeding heavily, answered solemnly:

'*If you don't believe it, then it's up to you. But I tell you that raven you knocked about is going to bring a curse on you.*'

Zuzé Paraza's reminder was ill advised. The Indian set to work with his fists again. Two punches found their target, three missed. Zuzé's resistance grew even feebler. The alcohol in his bloodstream hampered his ability to dodge. Finally, a straight left caught Zuzé off balance and sent him crashing to the floor on top of the raven. Covered in dust, Zuzé Paraza pulled the dead bird from under him. Then raising the magic raven, he brandished it in front of the Indian.

'*You've killed the bird, Sulemane! You're done for. You'll see what's going to happen to you! You're going to crawl around on all fours like a pig!*'

Then, the unbelievable happened. Sulemane began to quiver, to grunt and snort, and foam at the mouth. Falling to his knees, he dragged his belly along the ground, and rolled in the sand. The terrified onlookers took to their heels: Zuzé's curse had come true. Sulemane twitched convulsively like a chicken when it has had its head cut off. Finally, he stopped, weary of the demons which had shaken him. Zuzé knew that the next thing he would feel would be thirst. Seeing his opportunity, he commanded:

'You are going to feel thirsty, you great porcupine! You're going to cry out for water!'

There was proof of Zuzé's power: Sulemane begging for water on bended knee, beseeching them to kill the thirst that was killing him.

The news went through the village like a lightning flash. So it was true, after all, about this fellow Zuzé. He really did have a sorcerer's power. The following day, everyone got up early. They ran to Zuzé Paraza's house. Everybody wanted to see the painter, all wanted to ask him a favour, to bless them with good fortune.

When they arrived, they found the house empty. Zuzé Paraza had left. They scanned the horizon for some sign of the soothsayer, but their gaze perished in the distant grass where the crickets are quiet. They searched the abandoned house. The old man had taken all his things. All that remained was a cage hanging from the ceiling. It rocked gently to and fro, a widowed guest of the surrounding silence. With fear gradually mounting within them, the visitors went out to the back. It was there, in the yard, that they saw evidence of the curse: a dead bird, as yet unburied. Over that still scene, a breeze began to blow which little by little detached the talking raven's scrawny feathers from its carcass and cast them into the air.

Believing this omen, the inhabitants began to abandon the village. Some left in groups, others alone, and for many days they drifted aimlessly like the feathers that the wind slowly scattered in the distance.

The Day Mabata-bata Exploded

Suddenly, the ox exploded. It burst without so much as a moo. In the surrounding grass a rain of chunks and slices fell, as if the fruit and leaves of the ox. Its flesh turned into red butterflies. Its bones were scattered coins. Its horns were caught in some branches, swinging to and fro, imitating life in the invisibility of the wind.

Azarias, the little cowherd, could not contain his astonishment. Only a moment before, he had been admiring the great speckled ox, Mabata-bata. The creature grazed more slowly than laziness itself. It was the largest in the herd, ruler of the horned fraternity, and it was being kept aside as a bride price for its owner, Uncle Raul. Azarias had been working for him ever since he had been left an orphan. He would get up when it was still dark so that the cattle might graze the early morning mist.

He surveyed the disaster: the ox pulverised, like an echo of silence, a shadow of nothingness.

'It must have been a lightning flash.' he thought.

But it couldn't have been lightning. The sky was clear, blue without the slightest smudge. Where could the bolt have come from? Or was it the earth which had flashed?

He questioned the horizon beyond the trees. Perhaps the *ndlati*, the bird of lightning, was still circling the skies. He turned his gaze towards the mountain in front of him. It was there that the *ndlati* dwelt, there where all the rivers are one, born from the same desire to be water. The *ndlati* lives concealed in its four colours and only takes to the air when the clouds bellow and the sky grates. Then it is that the *ndlati* rises into the heavens on the wings of its madness. High in the air, it dons its clothes of flame, and casts its burning flight upon the creatures of the earth. Sometimes it throws itself to the ground, making a hole. It remains in the cavity and urinates there.

Once upon a time it was necessary to resort to the skills of the old medicine man to dig out that nest and retrieve its acid deposits. Maybe Mabata-bata had trodden on some malign vestige of the *ndlati*. But who would believe it? Not his uncle. He would want to see the dead ox, at least be shown some proof of the accident. He had already seen thunderstruck cattle: they became burnt out carcasses, a pattern of ashes reminiscent of a body. Fire chews slowly, it doesn't swallow in one go, which is what had happened here.

He looked about him: the rest of the cattle had scattered into the bush in fright. Fear slid from the little cowherd's eyes.

'Don't come back without an ox, Azarias. That's all I say: you'd better not come back.'

His uncle's threat blustered in his ears. That anxiety consumed the air he breathed. What could he do? Thoughts rushed at him like shadows but found no way out of the problem. There was only one solution: to run away, to travel the roads where he knew nothing more. To flee is to die from a place and, with his torn trousers, an old bag over his shoulder, what would he leave behind to regret? Mistreatment, running after cattle. Other people's children were allowed to go to school. Not he, for he was nobody's son. Work tore him early from his bed and returned him to sleep when there was no longer any trace of childhood left in him. He only played with animals: swimming the river clinging to the tail of Mabata-bata, making bets when the stronger animals fought each other. At home, his uncle told his fortune:

18

'*This one, judging by the way he lives mixed up with livestock, will surely marry a cow.*'

And everyone laughed, without a care for his tiny soul, his mistreated dreams. This was why he looked back at the fields he was going to leave behind without any regrets. He considered the contents of his bag: a catapult, some *djambalau* fruit, a rusty penknife. So little cannot inspire any remorse. He set off in the direction of the river. He felt he was not running away: he was merely starting out along his road. When he arrived at the river he crossed the frontier of water. On the other bank, he stopped without even knowing what he was waiting for.

As evening fell, Grandmother Carolina was waiting for Raul at the door of the house. When he arrived, she let fly with her anxieties:

'*So late, and Azarias hasn't come back with the cattle.*'

'*What? That brat is going to get a good hiding when he gets back.*'

'*Isn't it that something has happened, Raul? I'm scared, these bandits . . .*'

'*Some fun and games have happened, that's what.*'

They sat on the mat and had dinner. They talked about the matter of the bride price, the wedding preparations. Suddenly, there was a knock at the door. Raul got up, casting Grandmother Carolina a questioning glance. He opened the door: they were soldiers, three of them.

'*Good evening, do you want something?*'

'*Good evening. We've come to inform you of an incident: a mine exploded this afternoon. An ox trod on it. Now, that ox belonged here.*'

Another soldier added: '*We want to know where its minder is.*'

'*The minder's the one we're waiting for,*' Raul answered. And shouted: '*These bloody bandits!*'

'*When he arrives, we want to talk to him, to find out how it was that it happened. Nobody should go out towards the mountain. The bandits have been laying mines over there.*'

They left. Raul remained, hovering round his questions.

19

Where's that son-of-a-bitch Azarias gone? And was the rest of the herd scattered out there goodness knows where?

'Grandmother: I can't stay here like this. I've got to go and see where that good-for-nothing has got to. It must be that he's let the herd scatter maybe. I must round up the cattle while it's still early.'

'You can't, Raul. Look at what the soldiers said. It's dangerous.'

But he disregarded her and went off into the night. Does the bush have a suburb? It does: it was where Azarias had taken the animals. Raul, tearing himself on the thorns, could not deny the boy's skill. Nobody could match him in his knowledge of the land. He calculated the little cowherd would have chosen to take refuge in the valley.

He reached the river and climbed the big rocks. At the top of his voice, he issued his command:

'Azarias, come back, Azarias!'

Only the river answered, disentombing its gushing voice. Nothingness all around. But he sensed his nephew's hidden presence.

'Show yourself, don't be scared. I shan't hit you, I promise.'

He promised lies. He wasn't going to hit him: he was going to thrash him to death, when he had finished rounding up the cattle. For the time being he decided to sit down, a statue of darkness. His eyes, now used to the half light, disembarked on the other bank. Suddenly, he heard footsteps in the bush. He stood on his guard.

'Azarias?'

It wasn't him. Carolina's voice reached Raul's ears.

'It's me, Raul.'

Curse that old hag, what did she want? To interfere, that's all. She might tread on a mine and blow herself up and, worse still, him too.

'Go back home, Grandmother!'

'Azarias will refuse to hear you when you call. He'll listen to me though.'

20

And she put her assuredness into effect by calling the cowherd. From behind the shadows, a silhouette appeared.

'*Is that you Azarias? Come with me, let's go home.*'

'*I don't want to. I'm going to run away.*'

Raul began to creep down the rock, cat-like, ready to pounce and seize his nephew by the throat.

'*Where are you going to run away to, child?*'

'*I've nowhere to go, Grandmother.*'

'*That fellow's going to come back even if I have to cudgel him back in little pieces,*' Raul's guileful voice cut in quickly.

'*Be quiet, Raul. In your life you don't know the meaning of wretchedness.*' And turning to the cowherd: '*Come my child, I'll look after you. It wasn't your fault that the ox died. Come and help your uncle to herd the animals.*'

'*There's no need. The cattle are here, alongside me.*'

Raul stood up, unsure. His heart began to do a drum dance inside his chest.

'*What's that? The cattle are there?*'

'*Yes, that's right.*'

The silence became twisted and tangled. Azarias's uncle was not sure of his nephew's truth.

'*Nephew, did you really do it? Did you round up the cattle?*'

The grandmother smiled, thinking of how the quarrels of the two of them would now end. She promised him a reward and asked the boy to choose.

'*Your uncle is very pleased. Choose. He will respect your request.*'

Raul thought it better to agree to everything at that moment. Later, he would correct the boy's illusions, and his sense of duty as a cowherd would return.

'*Tell us your wish then.*'

'*Uncle, next year can I go to school?*'

He had guessed this would be it. There was no way he would consent to this. By allowing him to go to school he would lose a minder for his oxen. But the occasion required bluff and he spoke with his back to his thoughts:

21

'Yes, you can go.'

'Really, Uncle?'

'How many mouths do you think I have?'

'I can continue to help with the cattle. School is only in the afternoon.'

'That's right. But we'll talk about all that later. Come on out of there.'

The little cowherd emerged from the shadow and ran along the sand to where the river offered him passage. Suddenly, there was an explosion and a flash which seemed to turn night into the middle of its day. The little cowherd swallowed all that red, the shriek of crackling fire. Amid the flecks of night he saw the *ndlati*, bird of lightning, swoop down. He tried to shout:

'Who are you coming to get, ndlati?'

But he spoke not a word. It wasn't the river that drowned his words: he was a fruit drained of sounds, pains and colours. Round about, everything began to close in, even the river sacrificed its water's life, and the world engulfed its floor in white smoke.

'Are you going to land on Grandmother, poor thing, so kind? Or have you chosen my uncle, after all repentant and full of promises like the true father who died on me?'

And before the bird of fire could decide, Azarias ran and embraced it in the passage of its flame.

The Birds of God

Begging your pardon, I don't know anything more like a pilgrim than the river. The waves pass by on a journey which has no end. For how long has it been water's job to do that? Alone in his old dugout, Ernesto Timba measured his life. At the age of twelve he had entered the school of pulling fish from the water. Ever in the waft of the current, his shadow had reflected the laws of the river dweller for the last thirty years. And what was it all for? Drought had exhausted the earth, the seeds were not fulfilling their promise. When he returned from fishing, he had nothing to defend himself from his wife and children, who impaled him with their eyes. Eyes like those of a dog, he was loath to admit, but the truth is that hunger makes men like animals.

While he contemplated his suffering, Timba made his craft glide slowly along. Under the *mafurreira* tree, there on the bank where the river narrows, he brought the boat to rest so that he might drive away his sad thoughts. He allowed his paddle to nibble the water and the dugout clung to the stillness. But he could not stop his thoughts:

'What life have I lived? Water, water, just nothing else.'

As it rocked to and fro, the dugout caused his anguish to multiply.

'One day they'll fish me out of the water, swallowed up by the river.'

He foresaw his wife and children watching him being pulled

from the mud, and it was as if the roots of the water were being torn up.

Overhead, the *mafurreira* retained the sun's fierce dispatch. But Timba wasn't listening to the tree, his eyes were peeping into his soul. And it was as if they were blind, for pain is a dust which drains light away. Still higher above, morning called and he caught the smell of the intense blue.

'*If only I belonged to the sky,*' he sighed.

And he felt the burden of thirty years of tiredness upon his life. He remembered the words of his father, uttered to teach him courage:

'*See the hunter there, what he does? He prepares his spear the moment he sees the gazelle. But the fisherman can't see the fish inside the river. The fisherman believes in something he can't see.*'

That was the lesson of the bound-to-be of life and he now recalled those wise words. It was getting late and hunger told him it was time to go home. He began to move his arm while casting a last glance upwards, beyond the clouds. It was then that a huge bird passed over the sky. It was like a king, pleased with its own majesty. The creature, high on the wing, held his eyes and an uncanny anxiety took root within him. He thought:

'*If that bird were to fall on my canoe now!*'

He uttered these words aloud. Hardly had he finished speaking than the bird shook its huge wings and quickly flew in a downward spiral towards the boat. It fell as if expelled from life. Timba picked up the damaged bird and holding it in his hands, saw that the blood had not yet unbuttoned its body. In the boat, the animal gradually recovered, until it stood up and climbed onto the prow to take stock of its survival. Timba grabbed it, and weighed its flesh in order to work out how many meals it would provide. He put the idea out of his mind, and with a shove, helped the bird to take off.

'*Be off with you bird, go back from where you came!*'

But the bird turned round and headed back to the boat. The

24

fisherman once again drove it away. Yet again it returned. Ernesto Timba began to despair.

'Get back to your life, you bloody bird.'

Nothing. The bird didn't move. It was then that the fisherman began to wonder: that thing wasn't a bird, it was a sign from God. The warning from heaven would destroy his peace of mind forever.

Accompanied by the animal, he returned to the village. His wife celebrated his homecoming:

'Let's have the bird for lunch!'

Delighted, she called the children:

'Little ones, come and see the dicky-bird.'

Without answering, Timba placed the bird on the mat and went to the back of the house to fetch some wooden boards, wire and reeds. Then he set to work to build a cage so large that even a man could fit inside standing up straight. He put the animal inside and fed it the fish he had caught.

His wife was flabbergasted: the man was mad. Time passed and Timba only cared about the bird.

His wife would ask, pointing at the bird:

'Seeing as how hunger is pinching us, don't you want to kill it?'

Timba would raise his arm, emphatically. *'Never! Whoever touched the bird would be punished by God, would be marked down for life.'*

And so the days passed by, while the fisherman awaited fresh signs of divine intentions. Countless times he lingered in the moist afternoon heat while the river sat there in front of him. When the sun went down, he would go and check the cage where the animal was growing ever fatter. Little by little, he began to notice a shadow of sadness fall over the sacred bird. He realised the creature was suffering because it was lonely. One night he asked God to send the solitary fowl a companion. The following day, the cage had a new inmate, a female. Timba silently thanked the heavens for this new gift. At the same time, anxiety took root in him: why had God entrusted him to keep these animals? What might be the message they brought?

He thought and thought. That sign, that lightning flash of white plumage could only mean that heaven's humour was about to change. If men would agree to dispense their kindness to those messengers from heaven, then the drought would end and the season of rains would begin. It had befallen him, a poor fisherman of the river, to play host to God's envoys. It was his task to show that men could still be good. Yes, that true goodness cannot be measured in times of abundance but when hunger dances in the bodies of men.

His wife, who had returned from the *machamba**, interrupted his thoughts:

'So there are two of them now, are there?'

She came over, sat down on the same mat and looking long and hard into her companion's eyes, said:

'Husband, the pot's on the fire. I'm asking you for the neck of one of them, just one.'

It was a waste of time. Timba promised severe punishment to whoever mistreated the divine birds.

In time, the couple had chicks. There were three of them, clumsy and ugly, their gullets ever open: enough appetite to empty the river. Timba toiled on behalf of their parents. The household provisions, already so scarce, were diverted to feed the coop.

In the village, the rumour went around: Ernesto Timba was stark raving mad. His own wife, after many a threat, left home taking with her all the children. Timba didn't even seem to notice his family's absence. He was more concerned with ensuring his poultry's protection. He detected a spirit of envy around him, vengeance hatching itself. Was it his fault that he had been chosen? They said he had gone crazy. But he who is chosen by God always wanders off his path.

*Small plot of land for cultivation.

26

Then, one afternoon, when he had finished his work on the river, a feeling of uncertainty set his mind aflame: the birds! He set off home at a rush. When he got near, he saw a pall of smoke rising through the trees around his house. He paddled his dugout towards the river bank, jumped out without even tying it up, and began to run towards the scene of the tragedy. When he arrived, all he saw was wreckage and ashes. The wood and wire had been chewed up by the flames. From between the boards a wing, untouched by the fire, sought to save itself. The bird must have hurled itself against the wall of flames and the wing had got away, an arrow ominously pointing towards disaster. It was not swaying to and fro, as is the obsession of dead things. It was rigid, full of certainty.

Timba stepped back, appalled. He shouted for his wife, for his children, and then, on discovering that there was nobody else to shout for, he wept such copious tears of rage that his eyes hurt.

Why? Why had they harmed those birds, pretty as they were? And there and then, amidst all the ash and the smoke, he addressed himself to God:

'You're going to be angry, I know. You're going to punish your children. But look: I'm asking you to forgive them. Let me be the one to die, me. Leave the others to suffer what they are already suffering. You can forget the rain even, you can leave the dust lying on the ground, but please don't punish the men of this land.'

The following day, they found Ernesto hugging the current of the river, chilled by the early morning mist. When they tried to raise him, they found him heavy and impossible to separate from the water. The strongest men were brought to the task, but their efforts were in vain. The body was stuck to the surface of the river. A strange feeling of dread spread among those present. To hide their fear, someone said:

'Go and tell his wife. Tell the others that the village madman has died.'

And they withdrew. As they were climbing the bank, the clouds clashed, the sky seemed to cough sullenly as if it were

27

sick. In different circumstances, they would have celebrated the coming of the rain. Not now. For the first time, their faiths joined together pleading that it might not rain.

Impassive, the river flowed on into the distance, laughing at the ignorance of men. Ernesto Timba, gently lulled by the current, was carried downstream, and shown the by-ways he had only glimpsed in dreams.

How Ascolino Do Perpétuo Socorro
Lost His Spouse

Vivenda da Santíssima Palha was the name on the sign by the side of the road. A path of sand led to the farm, a place which no longer knew the meaning of sweat and toil. In the middle, half hidden by mango trees, the colonial farmhouse measured itself against time. There, in the afternoon shade, Ascolino Fernandes do Perpétuo Socorro would relax on the veranda. Inheritor of the estate, he ruminated over memories, unhurried and without obligations. He recalled Goa, his native land. He rejected the Mozambican in him:

'I am indeed an Indo-Portuguese, Catholic in my faith and in my customs.'

His dress was of the most formal kind, a suit of white linen, shoes of an identical whiteness, and hat of the selfsame colour. Ceremonious, correct, Ascolino embroidered his speech with the brocades of old Portugal which he admired so much. He decorated his repartee with adverbs for no reason or purpose. A long list of them introduced sentences which were spoken incorrectly and with a strong accent:

'Notwithstanding, however, nevertheless, perforce . . .'

In Munhava he had established his domains, more dreamt of than firmly fixed. He alone discerned the glory of being Goan, while separating the breeze from the flies during the long afternoons.

He bowed to his visitors, bestowing upon them long silences and green mangoes with salt. Dona Epifânia, his wife, was the

29

one who served them, so thin that one was not even aware she was approaching. When the net doors flapped, one knew she was there. No one had ever witnessed any expression of love pass between them. Did they love each other? If so, they loved without their bodies. Ascolino suffered because of his wife's constant seclusion. He consoled himself but without conviction. Epifânia, he was wont to say, is a clam. If opened, it dies, exposed to the air and to the tides. When the others noted his wife's absence, Ascolino would affirm:

'*Epifane, most sacred spouse indeed. Notvitsanding, howevah, darty years of marriage.*'

Five o'clock in the afternoon was a venerated hour, even more sacred than his wife. Whether or not there were visitors, the ritual was repeated. Vasco João Joãoquinho, faithful and devoted servant, would emerge from the shadow of the mango trees. He wore a khaki uniform which consisted of a tunic and neatly pressed trousers. He would approach, wheeling a bicycle. Ascolino Fernandes, with his eye for protocol, would salute both present and absent friends. The servant would hand him a little cushion which he would arrange on the bicycle frame. He would climb on taking great care not to dirty his trousers on the chain. With these preparations now complete, Vasco João Joãoquinho would mount the saddle, and with a vigorous shove, begin the pageant. Their sally was made all the more difficult by the undulations in the sand. And the two of them, Ascolino and his bicycle chauffeur would press on bound for Meneses's bottle store dispensing greetings as they went. The movements of both were correct, only their vehicle did not uphold the by-laws. On they would press, obeying the degenerate will of Ascolino, pedalling against thirst and distance.

On that afternoon the same scenery passed by with the same men inside it. Vasco chose the grassy parts of the track so the tyres gripped better. Suddenly, the bicycle keeled over and both master and servant fell into the ditch. Ascolino lay motionless

30

in the mud. Vasco picked up the bits and pieces, straightened the handlebars and brushed down his master's hat.

Ascolino recomposed himself with some difficulty. He surveyed the damage and began to chide his servant:

'What have you done, man? You have been spoiling our hat indeed. Who will pay for it perforce?'

'Sorry, boss. I was trying to steer the bicycle clear of that mud back there.'

'Are you not seeing, fellow? I am always telling you: do not brake so suddenly.'

And on they climbed again: Ascolino Perpétuo Socorro, his dignity restored, his hat battered, Vasco pedalling through the sunset. Overhead, the coconut palms lent sound to the breeze.

'Try not to derail the velocipede again, Vasco, will you?'

Reeling through the sands, the servant pushed with all the strength of his legs. But the Goan's thirst could not wait for the minutes to go by:

'Proceed post-haste, Vasco. Pedal harder!'

They arrived at the Bar Viriato, Meneses's store. The bicycle came to a halt by the cement-paved frontage. The master climbed off, brushing the dust off his clothes. He pulled out his pocket watch as he made his way towards his reserved table. Vasco did not enter the front part. Blacks, according to the custom of the time, were only admitted at the rear. In the back yard watered down wine was served. In the bar, in front, the quality was of a different order.

Vasco João Joãoquinho took his time coming in. The others greeted his arrival and asked for stories about him and his boss Ascolino. Vasco always had a tale to tell, inventing amusing incidents. But he always lingered over the beginning while preparing the condiments of the adventure.

'Well now, Vasco? What happened last night with your boss?'

31

Vasco considered his words, and chuckled as he thought ahead about the tale he was going to tell.

'*You won't believe this one about my boss . . .*'

'*Come on, man! Tell us it.*'

And he related the incredible incident of the previous night. Ascolino Fernandes, in the furthest depths of the middle of the night, had started his singsong with the *Fado* of the Little Swallows*. Vasco Joãoquinho imitated him, glass in hand:

> '*When a little swallow died*
> *All the little girls cried . . .*'

Ascolino sang the whole night through. The little swallows kept dying and his fury kept growing. Until he began to trumpet threats through the open window:

'*Now, I'm going to throw the fan out.*'

And crashing down came the fan, hurled from the first floor. It smashed into smithereens on the ground, its pieces flying across the yard. Then, another warning:

'*Now for the dishes.*'

And down into the garden fell pieces of crockery. Gleaming splinters of glass exploded into a thousand moons in the yard of the farmhouse. Ascolino sang ever louder:

> '*When a little swallow died . . .*'

There was no sign of Epifânia. Maybe she was shut away in her room. Or perhaps she was crying in the way that only she knew how. The saddest sadness is that which is not heard.

'*I'm talking seriously, my friends, because I know all about sadness. Our race cries with its body. They don't. They're locked inside their tribulations.*'

'*Listen here, Vasco, don't get off the subject. Go on with the story about your boss.*'

*A type of popular song from Portugal.

Bits of furniture came travelling through the window. Vasco came over and begged:

'*Please, boss, stop all this.*'

'*Get out of the way, Vasco.*'

'*Oh boss, don't go on, don't wreck the whole house.*'

'*Whose house is it? Is it yours?*'

'*But, boss, have you seen all the junk down here?*'

'*Get out of the way! Hurry! Now, I am throwing the fridge machine.*'

Terrified, Vasco left the yard. Taking a short step and then a longer one to avoid the broken glass, the servant went and hid in the shadows. There, sheltered by the darkness, he waited for the crash. Nothing. The refrigerator wasn't coming.

'*Boss?*'

'*What is it that you are wanting? Nevertheless are you still annoying me?*'

Then he began to sing *fados* again. He bellowed his song, the whole of Munhava was littered with little swallows. He interrupted his artistry and turned towards the inside of the house to insult Epifânia:

'*You don't care about me. It's just prayers from morning to night. This isn't a house for mortals. It's not a farmhouse! It's a church. The Cathedral of Santíssima Palha. Notwithstanding, I tell you what I am going to do: I am going to throw out all the furniture for praying, your crucifix and the altar. Everything out, out of here!*'

Then it was the turn of silence. Vasco Joãoquinho asked himself: is this an interval or the end of the show? Just as he thought it was all over, he heard the noise of a chair being dragged over to the window. It was then that the figure of the Goan appeared fully, from his knees to his head. His skinny hands tidied his unkept appearance while he announced solemnly:

'*The furniture has all gone. Now it is my turn.*'

And before Vasco could say anything, Ascolino Fernandes do Perpétuo Socorro threw himself down from the window. Ascolino's skinniness did not help his speed. He was more like a curtain than a body. When he landed, he didn't get so much as a grunt from the ground. Just a sigh, a little cloud of dust. Vasco, alarmed, ran over to help. He searched for signs of blood, of injury to the body. There were none.

'*Boss, did you damage anything.*'

'*What anything? Help me out of the ground.*'

He lifted his boss. When he had reached his full height, Ascolino surveyed the damage around him. Then he walked away through the darkness quietly humming his *fado*.

Everyone at the rear of the Bar Viriato laughed at the story. This time, however, Vasco Joãoquinho arranged his silence with an expression of sadness on his face.

'*Hey, Vasco, you always bring us such good stories, man.*'

'*I didn't invent it. All of what I told you happened. But don't laugh so loud, he might be listening from over the other side.*'

But nothing could be heard from the other side. Ascolino was hard at work on the whisky. Separated by only a wall, the other side was still a long way away.

Seated at his reserved table, Ascolino, relishing his own company, recalled Goa, Damão and Diu and spouted adverbs. Notwithstanding, however.

'*Please to bring me another helping of visky.*'

Meneses didn't even seem to see Ascolino. He poured out the orders while the sky gradually lost its light. Time slipped by between one glass and another. Ascolino drank with the confidence of a viceroy of the Indies. A finer quality Ascolino than the other Ascolino – the Indo-Portuguese superimposing himself on the Mozambican by means of alcohol. Only one anxiety remained which had not been drowned by whisky: Epifânia. At this stage, his wife must be turning in her sleep, tossed between insults and exhaustion. Ascolino looked at the time, he didn't want to stop for the night on the journey home. Guessing his fears, a Portuguese said:

'*Don't hurry yourself, Fernandes. Don't hurry. Your lady's going to get angry with you anyway.*'

Ascolino decided to ignore deadlines, to show he was a man, and daring in his delay. If he was downtrodden in life, he excelled in the art of discourse.

'*Epifane, she is already being aware of everything. Curry,* chacuti, sarapatel, *all the good food there is, everything she has been cooking for us to eat upon our arrival. Epifane, most sacred spouse.*'

At another table, a group of soldiers awaited their chance. At this point they decided to issue their challenge:

'*Goa's gone. Indian mother-fuckers; scum of the earth.*'

But Ascolino, to their astonishment, did not show offence. On the contrary, he joined his assailants.

'*Yes sir, Indian mother-fuckers indeed. Perforce, however, I am an Indo-Portuguese, defender of the Lusitanian fatherland against its enemies.*'

The soldiers eyed each other suspiciously. But Ascolino took the affirmation of his Portuguese loyalty a step further. He climbed onto his chair and swaying this way and that, held forth upon his heroic dreams. A crusade, yes, a crusade to reconquer the name of Goa for Portuguese usage. At its head, commanding the battalions, he, Ascolino Fernandes do Perpétuo Socorro. Behind him, soldiers and missionaries, ships loaded with arms, bibles and some little bottles of visky.

'*This bloke's taking the piss out of us,*' concluded one of the soldiers, the biggest one. He got up and walked over to Ascolino, getting the scent of his humours:

'*Crusades, what crusades? The only cross you carry is the cross your crossed legs make, your skinny little darkie's legs.*'

It was not intentional, perhaps it was because he lost his balance, but Ascolino spilled a few drops of whisky on the other man's uniform. A fist flew through the air, tore through the orator's words and Ascolino collapsed on the ground. The others seized the aggressor, dragged him away, and threw him out of the bar. Ascolino lay there on his back, in surrogate death, one arm raised and holding his glass. Meneses came to his assistance:

'*Senhor Ascolino, are you all right?*'
'*I have been fallen flat.*'
'*But how did it happen?*'
'*Abruptly.*'

They put the Goan back on his feet. He straightened his creases, and peered into the bottom of his glass. He looked round at the crowd and declared the crusade postponed.

In front of the bar, the Goan prepared his retreat:

'*Vashcooo, lessgo!*'

While waiting for his chauffeur, he fumbled for his pocket watch, creature of habit that he was. But this time he found the chain, but no watch. Ascolino consulted his non-existent watch and remarked on the lateness of the hour.

'*Quick-ly, Vashcooo.*'

He arranged the cushion on the bicycle frame before seating himself. The cushion was in place, it was just that Ascolino missed. He fell, tried again, and returned to the ground.

'*Vashcooo, switch on the light, switch off this darkness.*'

The servant aligned the dynamo with the wheel and gave the pedal a healthy kick. Ascolino was on his hands and knees looking for his own body.

'*Did my hat run away?*'

Vasco Joãoquinho was also reeling. He picked up the hat and climbed on the bike. Then they both got ready, hindering each other in the process. Meneses enjoyed the spectacle from his window:

'*That darkie's stoned out of his mind. Full of whisky and punches.*'

Vasco pushed aside pieces of darkness and other obstacles as they set off home. He pedalled along, ringing his bell, *cring, cring*. No longer could ravens be heard or herons seen. Night had levelled colours, erased differences. As they went on, the effects of the Scottish brew began to be felt even more strongly by the Goan, who abandoned his good behaviour once and for all.

36

'*I'm a pale-arsed little darkie, a first-class one if you please.*' And shouting with all his soul: '*Long live Nehru!*'

Some way further on, where the rice plantations end and the coconut palms begin, Ascolino exchanged his servant for his wife and began to call him Epifânia.

'*A woman doesn't ride behind. Get up in front.*'

Vasco obediently gave up his saddle seat. The Goan, excited, grabbed his servant round the waist.

'*Hey boss, get away with you.*'

But Ascolino pressed forward with sugary insistence. He tried to kiss his servant who avoided him vigorously. As insistence increased, respect diminished. Vasco now pushed his boss aside:

'*Leave me alone, I'm not your woman.*' And another stronger shove sent Ascolino to the ground. Silence among the coconut groves. Only the ravens watched the scuffle inquisitively. The Goan lay spread-eagled on the ground. He asked for a light to see whether the stain on his trousers was puddle water, or whether he'd pissed in his pants. Vasco laughed. Ascolino began to raise himself, reeling, his nose nearly scraping the ground. Then, when finally upright, he examined the surrounding grass:

'*Vashcooo, they've stolen the Vivenda da Santíssima Palha!*'

'*No, boss! We haven't got there yet, there's still some way to go.*'

But Ascolino's mind was made up, and he retorted:

'*Vashcooo, we've lost the house. Perforce, you are going to look for it.*'

The servant lost his patience and began to pull him along by the armpits. On tow in this fashion, Ascolino saw the road back to front, retreating crab-like. Confusing his coming with his going, he pleaded:

'*Vashcooo, don't walk backwards. We are going back to Meneses's store.*'

And as if going on ahead, he shouted his order:

'*Meneses, give me visky, and another helping for Epifane, most holy drink.*'

37

And in a generous mood, he turned his head:

'*Order whatever you want, Vashcooo. And deduct it from your month's pay. You can drink on this side, there's no need for you to go to the back.*'

Tired out with walking backwards, Vasco let go of him. Feeling himself horizontal, the Goan said his prayers and then took his leave:

'*Good night, Epifane, most holy wife.*'

But Vasco was no longer there. He went back to get the bicycle. Ascolino raised his head with difficulty and seeing his servant loaded down, he hailed him:

'*That's it, bring my blanket to cover me with. And cover Epifane too.*'

Vasco, in despair, attempted a final warning:

'*I don't know, boss. If we don't get back tonight, and sleep here, your lady's going to kick up a big fuss.*'

Ascolino agreed. The threat seemed to have had an effect. Propping himself on his elbows, the boss looked straight at his servant and said:

'*What's wrong Epifânia? Are you sleeping in khaki trousers now?*'

And without further ado, he fell asleep. So heavy was his slumber that Vasco failed to budge him.

Next morning, they were covered by a sheet of insects, leaves and dew. Vasco was the first to arrive back in the world. He was surprised by the sound of a motor nearby. He looked around him, fighting the weight of his eyelids. It was then that he saw, in the near distance, the Vivenda da Santíssima Palha. Could it be that they had slept only a minute or two from home?

In the front yard, all the furniture had been piled up. There were men loading it all onto a lorry. That, then, was the motor he had heard. Dona Epifânia directed the operation like some supreme commander.

The servant hesitated. He looked at his boss, still given over to sleep. Finally, he made up his mind. Vasco Joãoquinho followed the familiar sandy path up to the house. When he got there, he realised what his mistress intended to do. She wanted to leave, to terminate her association with Ascolino without warning or explanation.

'*Senhora, don't go away, please.*'

The mistress was startled. Then, recovering from her fright, she continued with her removal.

'*Senhora, we were late because of the beating the boss got back there in the bar.*'

The words of the servant said nothing. His mistress continued to give out her orders. But Vasco Joãoquinho didn't give up:

'*Senhora, it wasn't just the business of the beating. We were late because of an accident on the road.*'

'*An accident?*'

Epifânia, suddenly uncertain, began to think. She asked for proof of his truth. Vasco showed her the twisted hat. She looked at the stains and bit her lip. She chose her words carefully before asking:

'*Was he killed?*'

'*Killed? No, Senhora. He's just lying in the road.*'

'*Is he hurt?*'

'*No, not at all. He's just sleepy. Can I go and get him?*'

Words to be regretted, for once Epifânia had heard them she renewed her determination to leave and the furniture began to be loaded again.

Vasco retraced his steps along the road. Slowly, he returned to the place where he had left his boss's sleep. When he got there, Ascolino was already stretching himself. Unable to take the light, he rubbed his eyes, unaware of the noise of the approaching lorry. He sat up and his aching body shrank. The lorry's horn startled him, and in one leap he landed in the ditch. The load passed slowly by, as if opposed to its journey. There before Ascolino's untutored eyes, his life was ebbing away, unrecorded and unnoticed. When the dust settled, Vasco could be seen standing glumly on one side of the road. On the other, Ascolino was climbing out of the ditch. As he looked, the lorry continued further into the distance. Then, brushing the creases in his coat, he asked:

'*What's happening Vasco? Are some neighbours moving from Munhava?*'

'*They're not neighbours, boss. It's the lady, Dona Epifânia herself who is going away.*'

'*Epifane?*'

'*Yes. And she's taking everything with her.*'

Ascolino looked askance, repeating:

'*Epifane?*'

He stood there churning over his thoughts, kicking at clumps of grass, untidying the scenery. The servant couldn't bring himself to look up. Then, suddenly, Ascolino spoke decisively:

'*Bring the bicycle, Vasco. We are going to pursue that lorry. Quickly.*'

'*But boss, the lorry's a long way ahead by now.*'

'*Quiet, you know-nothing. Load the velocipede, speedily.*'

So the servant prepared the seats. On the frame, and without a cushion, sat the boss, while the servant sat on the saddle. And they began to cycle off down the road.

The groove made by the tyre gradually unwove itself in the morning air. No longer could the noise of the lorry be heard through the surrounding rice fields. Ascolino the viceroy, led his impossible crusade to try and regain his lost spouse.

'*Pedal, pedal quickly. Perforce we must arrive early. When five o'clock strikes we must go back to Meneses's store.*'

So You Haven't Flown Yet, Carlota Gentina?

1. *Your honour, let me begin*

I are sad. No, I'm not mistaken. What I'm saying is correct. Or perhaps: we am sad? Because inside me, I'm not alone. I'm many. And they all fight over my one and only life. We go along reaping our deaths. But we only have one birth. That's where the problem lies. That's why, when I tell my story, I mix myself up, a mulatto not of races, but of existences.

They say I killed my wife. In real life, I killed one who didn't exist. She was a bird. I let her go when I saw that she didn't have a voice, that she was dying without so much as a complaint. What dumb creature was it that came out of her through the interval of her body?

Very well, your honour, you, a doctor of the laws, have asked me to write down my story, and that's what I'm going to do, a little bit every day. What I'm going to tell you, you're going to use to defend me in court. But you don't even know me. Does my suffering interest you, sir? It doesn't matter to me either. Here I am talking away about this and that, but I don't want anything, I don't want to get out any more than I want to stay. These six years that I've been locked up in this cell have been enough for me to unlearn my life. Now, sir, I just want to be dying. To die is for such a long time, living is too short. I'll stay in between. On my way to death. Do you think that's funny?

I'll explain: the dying are allowed to do what they want. No

41

one laughs at them. They anticipate respect for the dead, they are pre-deceased. When the dying insult us, we forgive them for sure. If they shit in their sheets or spit in their dinner plate, we clean up after them, no questions asked. Please, your honour, help me. Fix it so that I can be dying, sub-dead.

After all, here I am in this prison because I decided to become a prisoner. That's the plain truth, no one pointed the finger at me. Sick of myself, I informed against me. I gave myself up. Maybe on account of being tired of waiting for a time that never came. I can wait, but never get anything. When the future arrives it won't find me. When all is said and done, where am I? Isn't this time the place of my life?

I'm going to leave my thoughts to themselves, and get straight to the story. I'll begin with my brother-in-law Bartolomeu. The night he came looking for me, that was when disaster began to strike.

2. *Wings on the ground, embers in the sky*

Light was getting thin. Only a glassful of sky was left. In my brother-in-law Bartolomeu's house, they were preparing for the end of the day. He glanced round the hut: his wife bustled about causing the last shadows from the oil lamp to flicker. Then his wife went to bed, but Bartolomeu was restless. Sleep wouldn't come quickly to him. Outside an owl began to hoot calamities. His wife didn't hear the bird warning of death, she was already in the arms of sleep. Bartolomeu said to himself:

'I'm going to make tea: maybe that'll help me to sleep.'

The fire was still burning. He took a stick of wood and blew on it. He shook the crumbs of flame from his eyes and in the confusion dropped the lighted stick on his wife's back. The cry she let out no one had ever heard the likes of before. It wasn't the sound a person would make, it was the howl of an animal. A hyena's voice for sure. Bartolomeu jumped with fright: what am I married to then? a *nóii*? Those women who turn into animals at night and go around doing witches work?

His wife dragged her burning pain across the floor in front of his distress. Like an animal. What a luckless life, thought Bartolomeu. And he fled from home. He hurried across the village to tell me what had happened. He arrived at my house, and the dogs were very excited. He came in without knocking, without so much as an 'excuse me'. He told me his story just as I am writing it down. At first, I didn't believe him. Perhaps Bartolomeu had mixed his recollections up when drunk. I smelt the breath of his complaint. It didn't smell of drink. It was true then. Barolomeu repeated the story two, three, four times. I listened to it and thought to myself: and what if my wife is the same? What if she's a *nóii* too?

When Bartolomeu had left, the idea seized hold of my thoughts. And supposing I, without knowing it, were living with an animal-woman? If I had made love to her, then I had traded my human's mouth with an animal snout. How could I excuse such a trade? Were animals ever supposed to rest on a sleeping mat? Animals live and grow strong out in the corrals, beyond the wire. If that son-of-a-bitch of a woman had deceived me, I had become an animal myself. There was only one way to find out whether Carlota Gentina, my wife, was a *nóii* or not. It was to surprise her with some suffering, some deep pain. I looked around and saw a pot full of boiling water. I picked it up and poured the scalding liquid over her body. I waited for the scream but it didn't come. It didn't come at all. She just lay there crying silently, without making a noise. She was a curled up piece of silence there on the mat. All the following day she did not move. Poor Carlota was just a name lying on the ground. A name without a person: just a long, slow sleep inside a body. I shook her by the shoulders:

'Carlota, why don't you move? If you're in agony, why don't you scream?'

But death is a war of deceptions. Victories are just defeats

43

which have been put off. As long as life has a purpose to it, it will build a person. That's what Carlota was in need of: the lie of a purpose. I played the fool to make her laugh. I hopped round the mat like a locust. I clanked cooking pots against each other and spilt the noise over myself. Nothing. Her eyes remained glued to the far distance, gazing at the blind side of darkness. Only I laughed, wrapped up in my saucepans. I got up, breathless with laughter and went outside to give vent to my mad guffaws. I laughed until I was tired. Then gradually, I was overcome by sad thoughts, ancient pangs of conscience.

I went back inside and thought she would probably like to see the light of day, and stretch her legs. I took her outside. She was so light that her blood can have been no more than red dust. I sat Carlota down facing the setting sun. I let the fresh air soak her body. There, sitting in the back yard, my wife Carlota Gentina died. I didn't notice her death immediately. I only knew it when I saw the tear which had stopped still in her eyes. That tear was already death's water.

I stood looking at the woman stretched out in that body of hers. I looked at the feet, torn like the surface of the earth. They had walked so many paths that they had become like brothers to the sand. The feet of the dead are big, they grow on after death. While I measured Carlota's death I began to have my doubts: what illness was it that caused neither swelling nor cries of pain? Can hot water just stop someone's age just like that? This was the conclusion I drew from my thoughts: Carlota Gentina was a bird, of the type that lose their voice in a headwind.

3.   *Dreams of the soul awoke me from my body*

I dreamt of her. She was in the back yard, working at her pestle. Do you know what she was grinding? Water. She was

44

grinding water. No, it wasn't corn, or *mapira*,* or anything else. It was water, grains from heaven.

I drew near. She was singing a sad song, it seemed as if she were lulling herself to sleep. I asked the reason for her work.

'I'm grinding.'

'Are those grains?'

'They're your tears, husband.'

And so it was: I saw that there in that pestle was the origin of my suffering. I asked her to stop but my voice could no longer be heard. My throat had gone blind. Just the tonk-tonk-tonk of the pestle, pounding, pounding, forever pounding. Then slowly I began to realise that the noise was coming from my chest, that it was my heart punishing me. Do you think I'm inventing this? Anyone can invent. But from this cell, all I can see are the walls of life. I can feel a dream, a passing whiff of perfume. But I can't grab it. Now I've exchanged my life for dreams. It wasn't just tonight that I dreamt of her. The night before last, your honour, I even cried. It was because I witnessed my own death. I looked down the corridor and saw blood, a river of it. It was orphan blood. Without its father, which was my severed arm. Imprisoned blood like its owner. Condemned. I don't remember how it came to be severed. I have a darkened memory because of these countless nights I've drunk.

And do you know who it was that saved my spilt blood in that dream? It was she. She scooped up the blood with her ancient hands. She cleaned it, lovingly extracted the dirt. She put all the bits together and showed them the way back into my body. Then she called me by that name of mine which I have already forgotten because nobody calls me by it. Here I'm a number, my name is made of digits, not letters.

You asked me to confess truths, your honour. It's true I killed her. Was it a crime? Maybe, if that is what they say. But I fall ill with the uncertainty. I'm not one of those widowers who

*A variety of local corn.

45

buries his memories. They are rescued by oblivion. Death hasn't taken Carlota away from me. Now I know why: the dead are all born on the same day. Only the living have separate birthdays. Did Carlota fly? That time I spilled water over her, was it over the woman or the bird? Who can tell? Can you, your honour?

One thing I know for sure: she was left outside her coffin. Those who wept at the funeral were blind. I was laughing. It's true, I was laughing. Because inside the coffin they were weeping at, there was nothing. She had fled, saved by her wings. They saw me laughing like this, but they didn't get angry. They forgave me. They thought it was laughter of the sort which is not an enemy of sadness. Maybe it was sobbing in disguise, the sweat of suffering. And they prayed. As for me, I couldn't. After all, it wasn't a fully deceased dead woman lying there. Rather it was a piece of silence in the form of a beast, that's what it was.

4. *I shall learn to be a tree*

Writing has made me tired of letters. I'm going to finish in a minute. I don't need a defence any more, your honour. I don't want one. After all, I'm guilty. I want to be punished, I have no other wish. Not because of the crime, but because of my mistake. At the end I'll explain what this mistake was. Six years ago I gave myself up, I arrested me by myself. Now, I myself am condemning me.

I am grateful for everything, your honour. I took up your time, for no payment. You'll call me an ass. I know and accept it. But begging your pardon, your honour, what do you know about me? I'm not like others: I think about what I can put up with, not about what I need. What I can't manage has nothing to do with me. God's failing, not mine. Why didn't God create us already made? Finished, like an animal which, when it has been born, only has to grow. If God made us live why didn't he let us rule our lives?

As it is, even when we're white, we're black. With respect, your honour, you're black too, let me tell you. It's a defect in the race of mankind, this race of ours which is everybody's. Our voices, blind and broken, no longer have authority. We only give orders to the weak: women and children. Even they have begun to be slow to obey. The power of a minion is to make others feel even smaller, to tread on others just as he himself is trodden on by his superiors. Crawling, that's what the job of souls is. If they're used to the ground how is it that they can believe in heaven?

Unfinished, incomplete, that's what we are, and we come to our end when buried. It's worth it to be a plant, your honour. I'm even going to learn to be a tree. Or perhaps a little clump of grass, for a tree wouldn't fit in here. Why don't those witches I was talking about try and be plants, all green and quiet? If that had happened, I wouldn't have had to kill Carlota. All I'd have had to do would be to transplant her; there would be no crime, no guilt.

I'm only afraid of one thing: of cold. All my life I've suffered from cold. Ague of the soul, not the body, that's what I get. Even when it's hot I still get the shivers. Bartolomeu, my brother-in-law, used to say: *'Away from home it's always cold'*. That's true. But I, your honour, what home have I ever had? None. Bare earth, without a here or a where. In a place like that, with neither arrival nor departure, you need to learn to be clever. Not the cleverness they teach you at school. An all round cleverness, a cleverness with no fixed job in mind, no contract with anybody.

You can see from this last letter, your honour, that I've given up. Why am I like this? Because Bartolomeu visited me today and told me everything just as it really happened. Afterwards I realised my mistake. Bartolomeu came to my conclusion for me: his wife, my sister-in-law, wasn't a *nóii*. He got proof of this

47

over several nights. He spied on his wife to see is she had some other nocturnal occupation. Nothing, she hadn't. She neither crawled round on all fours nor flew off like a bird. And so Bartolomeu was able to prove that his wife was a person.

Then I began to think. If my wife's sister wasn't a *nóii*, then neither was my wife. Witchcraft is a vice of sisters, an illness they are born with. But how could I have guessed it by myself? I couldn't have, your honour.

I am a son of my own world. I want to be judged by other laws, beholden to my tradition. My mistake was not that I killed Carlota. It was that I surrendered my life to this world of yours which does not rest easy with mine. There, where I come from, they know me. There they can decide what my goodnesses are. Here, no one can. How can I be defended if I can't obtain the understanding of others? I'm sorry, your honour: justice can only be done where I belong. When all is said and done, only they can tell that I didn't know Carlota Gentina didn't have wings to fly away with.

Now it's too late. I only notice the time when it has already passed. I'm a blind man who sees many doors. I open the nearest one. I don't choose, my hand merely stumbles across a latch. My life isn't a path. It is a solid stone waiting to become sand. Very slowly, I'm becoming at one with the grains of the earth. When they decide to bury me I'll already be soil. Seeing as I had no advantage in life, this will be my privilege in death.

Saíde, The Bucket of Water

An afternoon of wood and zinc. Sloping roofs brushed by the mist. The watery eyelids of the afternoon seemed to release bats into the air.

In the cane shanty, the landscape was kissed only by death. Saíde was returning home, stumbling over his curses, dragged along by beer, poured down him all afternoon to console his despair.

'Friends? Hell, they're the first to leave a bloke in the shit!'

Bursts of laughter came from open doorways.

'That's right, laugh, you bastards.'

He fumbled in his pockets. Cigarettes: none. Matches: none. His hands impatiently searched his clothes. He felt like a smoke, he needed the strength of a cigarette, the security of pre-ordained gestures.

'Look at the Bucket of Water. His wife hasn't set foot out of the house ever since he took to drink.'

It wasn't true. Women always get the reward of being felt sorry for. Bloody neighbours. The nearest they come is when they want to take a look at your adversities. Apart from that nobody knows who they are.

He went into his house and closed the door. His hand lingered distractedly on the latch, while he gazed round at the emptiness. He remembered the times when he had first met her: those days of Júlia Timane were beautiful ones indeed!

That had been a long time ago. He was sitting by a bus stop

waiting for nothing in particular, in the way that only drunks wait. She had walked up and sat down beside him. The *capulana** she wore over her shoulders seemed scarcely enough for such abiding cold. They had started talking.

'*I'm Júlia, I'm from Macia.*'

'*Haven't you a husband?*'

'*I had one. For the moment I haven't.*'

'*How many husbands have you had?*'

'*Many. I have children too.*'

'*Where are these children?*'

'*They're not with me. Their fathers took them away.*'

He offered her his coat to protect her from the cold. She helped him to find his way home. But she had finished up by staying the night. And the other nights too.

When they discovered that he was going with her, they rebuked him. She was secondhand. He ought to choose an untouched woman, to be initiated by his body. He refused to listen. It was then that they began to call him Bucket of Water. Everywhere, his nickname substituted his real name. Water accepts any shape it is given, it hasn't a personality of its own.

In time he began to realise something was wrong: she wasn't giving him children. Nobody could know about this. A man may or may not have a beard. But he must beget children: they are a document which the respects demand to see.

One day he said to her:

'*We must have a son.*'

'*We can't, you know only too well.*'

'*We must find a way.*'

'*A way? How? If it's not my fault? They explained the problem at the hospital: you're the one who can't have children.*'

'*I'm not talking about whose fault it is. I've already studied the problem and I've found a solution: take on your fuel outside, woman.*'

'*I don't understand.*'

*A dress worn by women, akin to a sarong.

50

'I'm telling you: sleep with someone else. I shan't get angry. I just want a son, that's all.'

◇

That evening she went out. She came back very late. The following evening the same thing happened. This went on for many nights.

He asked: *'Isn't once enough?'*

'Don't you want a son? It's best to make sure.'

'Do whatever you think best. But quickly, for I don't want to be put to any shame.'

Júlia became pregnant. He rejoiced in the news. Those first weeks were very happy. Up until the time he woke her up in the middle of the night.

'Júlia. I want to know: who is the owner of this pregnancy?'

'Armando, you swore never to ask.'

'Now I want to know the name. You can't give birth without my knowing the truth about the father of this child.'

Júlia remained silent and settled down once again in bed. He shook her violently.

'Are you going to beat me up?' she asked in alarm.

'If you don't tell me, I will.'

'I won't be the only one to be beaten. You may harm your son.'

He looked at himself: he was on his knees, as if at prayers. A man who demands doesn't assume the position of those who beg. He got up and went to light the oil lamp. In the shadow he spoke to her more calmly:

'Sleep, Júlia, I don't want to hear the name. Even if I ask you for it again, you must never tell me who the person is.'

She smiled, turned down the sheet and showed him the full round moon of her belly.

'It's your son, Saíde. Yours.'

The child was born. It was then that he confirmed the suspicion of a feeling: the baby boy was a stranger, a scar on his honour. But a live scar, a whimpering testimony to his

51

inadequacies. Sometimes he loved him and the child was his. At others, the baby was an interloper who rebuffed him.

In the neighbourhood, no one suspected the identity of the father. But Saíde felt more and more insecure: he would look at the child and it seemed to him to know everything. He had wanted a son to hide his shame. Instead, he had a son who threatened his life's secret. The home became increasingly difficult to live in. He became jealous of the attentions his wife devoted to his little rival. The future perturbed him like a darkened road. He beat his wife more and more often, his drunken bouts became ever more frequent. He never hit the little boy. The beatings he wanted to give him were directed at the mother.

He felt the strength of the wind through the doorway and was jolted out of his memories. Every time he recollected, knives got to work in his soul. The past was forbidden to him. And all because of Júlia, that devil of a woman. He closed the door with the decisiveness of rage.

'*You whore!*'

And he set about her with kicks. He wanted to hurt her, to unload all the pain he felt onto her. Cooking pots fell making a loud din. He was undismayed: leaning over the bed he insulted her, spat on her, threatened to kill her stone dead. The neighbours, he already knew, would not come to the rescue. And that night, his fury was greater than ever. He was determined to beat her until she bled. He pulled his belt out and used it with such force of will that he lost his balance and fell over the table. Dishes and glasses were shattered, once again ripping through the silence of night.

Suddenly, he heard a noise at the door. When he looked, whoever it was had just come in. It was Severino, the district warden.

'*What do you want, Severino?*'

'*Calm down, Saíde. What's all this for?*'

He was breathing as if feeding many souls.

'*Sit down, Saíde.*'

He obeyed. With his sighs he quenched the fire in his soul.

'*Why are you always doing this? Have you ever heard of anybody beating a woman the way you do?*'

He did not answer. He was trying to dampen down the heat inside his breast. He remained like that for a few minutes until he answered:

'*I'm not hitting anyone.*'

Severino did not understand. It must be that he's pissed; he'll start talking about everything under the sun. Saíde insisted.

'*There's no one else in this house except for me.*'

Severino looked around him suspiciously. It was true, there wasn't anybody else.

'*You can search everywhere, Júlia isn't here, she went away long ago. I'm not beating anyone.*'

'*I'm sorry, Saíde. I thought . . .*'

And as he was at a loss for words, he decided to leave. He backed out as if the surprise were a snake threatening to attack him.

'*Severino?*'

'*Yes, I'm listening.*'

'*I don't know why I do this. It's so that you people should think she's still here. Nobody must know that I've been deserted. Every time I deliver a beating, there's no one behind all that noise. You all think she doesn't go out because of the shame she feels in front of her neighbours. As long as you don't . . .*'

Severino was in a hurry to get out. Saíde stood there, his arms hanging limply at his sides. It was as if his flesh had turned to wood and deep sadness had been chiselled into him. Severino went out, closing the door with the care one shows when not wanting to disturb a child's sleep.

Outside, a crowd awaited news. The warden, with a vague gesture, spread his voice around:

'*You can all go. Mama Júlia is well. She asks you to return to your homes and sleep soundly.*'

Someone protested:

'*But Severino . . . What happened then?*'

The warden, with an embarrassed smile, replied:

'*Come, my friend. You know what these women of ours are like.*'

The Whales of Quissico

He just sat there. That's all. Sat stock still, just like that. Time did not lose its temper with him. It left him alone. Bento João Mussavele.

But nobody worried about him. People would pass by and see that deep down he wasn't idle. When they asked what he was doing, the answer would always be the same:

'I'm taking a bit of fresh air.'

It must have really been very fresh when, one day, he decided to get up.

'I'm off.'

His friends thought he was going back home. That he had finally decided to work and start planting a *machamba**. The farewells began.

Some went as far as to contest him:

'But where are you going? Where you come from is full of bandits, man.'

But he did not pay them any attention. He had chosen his idea, and it was a secret. He confided it to his uncle.

'You know, uncle, there's such hunger back there in Inhambane. People are dying every day.'

And he shook his head as if commiserating. But it had nothing to do with sentiment: just respect for the dead.

'They told me something. That something is going to change my life.'

*Small plot of land for cultivation.

55

He paused, and straightened himself in his chair: *'You know what a whale is . . . well I don't know how . . .'*

'A whale?'

'That's what I said.'

'But what's a whale got to do with it?'

'Because one appeared at Quissico. It's true.'

'But there aren't any whales; I've never seen one. And even if one did appear, how would people know what the creature was called?'

'People don't know the name. It was a journalist who started spreading this story around about it being a whale or not a whale. All we know is that it's a big fish which comes to land on the beach. It comes from the direction of the night. It opens its mouth and, boy, if you could see what it's got inside . . . It's full of things. Listen, it's like a store, but not the ones you see nowadays. It's like a store from the old days. Full. I swear I'm being serious.'

Then, he gave details: people would come up to it and make their requests. Each one depending on what he needed, exactly so. All you had to do was ask, just like that. No formal requisitions or production of travel papers. The creature would open its mouth and out would come peanuts, meat, olive oil. Salt cod, too.

'Can you just imagine it? All a bloke would need is a van, he'd load the things, fill it up, drive it here to the city. Go back again. Just think of the money he'd make.'

His uncle laughed long and loud. It seemed like a joke.

'It's all pie in the sky. There is no whale. Do you know how the story began?'

He made no reply. It was a wasted conversation, but he kept up the good-mannered pretence of listening, and his uncle continued:

'It's those folk there who are hungry. Very hungry. They start inventing these apparitions, as if they were wizardry. But they're just figments of the imagination, mirages . . .'

'Whales,' corrected Bento.

He was unmoved. This doubting wasn't enough to make him

give up. He would go around asking, he would find a way of getting together some money. And he set about doing just that.

He spent the whole day wandering up and down the streets. He spoke to Aunt Justina who has a stall in the market and with Marito, who has a van for hire. Both were sceptical. Let him go to Quissico first and bring back some proof of the whale's existence. Let him bring back some goods, preferably some bottles of that water from Lisbon and then they might give him a hand.

Then one day he decided to seek better advice. He would ask the local wise men, that white, Senhor Almeida, and the black who went by the name of Agostinho. He began by consulting the black. He gave a brief outline of the matter in question.

'In the first place,' replied Agostinho, who was a schoolmaster, *'the whale is not what it seems at first sight. Whales are prone to deceive.'*

He felt a lump in his throat, as his hopes began to crumble.

'I've already been told that, Senhor Agostinho. But I believe in the whale; I have to believe in it.'

'That's not what I meant, my friend. I was trying to explain that the whale appears to be that which it isn't. It looks like a fish but it isn't one. It's a mammal. Just like you and me, for we are mammals.'

'So we are like the whale? Is that what you're saying?'

The schoolmaster spoke for half an hour. He made a great show of his Portuguese. Bento stood with his eyes wide open, avidly taking in the quasitranslation. But if the zoological explanation was detailed, the conversation did not satisfy Bento's intentions.

He tried the white man's house. He walked down the avenues lined with acacias. On the pavements, children played with the stamens of acacia flowers. Just look at it, everybody mixed together, white children and black. In the old days . . .

When he knocked at the wire mesh door of Almeida's residence, a housboy peeped through suspiciously. With a grimace he overcame the bright light outside, and when he saw the colour of the visitor's skin, he decided to keep the door closed.

'*I'm asking to speak to Senhor Almeida. He already knows me.*'

The conversation was brief, Almeida answered neither one way nor the other. He said the world was going crazy, that the earth's axis was more and more inclined and that the poles were becoming flatter, or flatulent, he didn't quite understand.

But that vague discourse gave him hope. It was almost like a confirmation. When he left, Bento was euphoric. He could see whales stretched out in rows as far as the eye could see, dozing on the beaches of Quissico. Hundreds of them, all loaded and he reviewing them from an MLJ station-wagon.

With the little money he had saved he bought a ticket and left. Signs of war could be seen all along the road. The charred remains of buses coupled with the wretchedness of the *machambas** punished by drought.

'*Now is it only the sun that rains?*'

The petrol fumes produced by the bus in which he was travelling seeped in among the passengers, who complained, but Bento Mussavele was miles away, already visualising the coast of Quissico. When he arrived, it all seemed familiar to him. The bay was fed by the waters from the lagoons of Massava and Maiene. That blue which melted away before one's eyes was beautiful. In the background, beyond the lagoons, there was land again, a brown strip which held the fury of the ocean in check. The persistence of the waves was gradually creating cracks in that rampart, embellishing it with tall islands which looked like mountains emerging from the blue in order to breathe. The whale would probably turn up over there, mingling with the grey of the sky at the end of the day.

He climbed down the ravine, his little satchel over his shoulder, until he reached the abandoned beach houses. In

---

*Small plot of land for cultivation.

times gone by, these houses had accommodated tourists. Not even the Portuguese used to go there. Only South Africans. Now, all was deserted and only he, Bento Mussavele, ruled over that unreal landscape. He settled in an old house, installing himself among the remains of furniture and the ghosts of a recent age. There he remained without being aware of the comings and goings of life. When the tide came in, no matter what the hour, Bento would walk down to the surf and stay there staring into the gloom. Sucking on an old unlit pipe, he brooded:

'It must come. I know it must come.'

Weeks later, his friends came to visit him. They risked the journey on one of Oliveira's buses, each bend in the road was a fright to ambush the heart. They arrived at the house after descending the slope. There was Bento slumbering amid aluminium camping dishes and wooden boxes. A tatty old mattress lay decomposing on a straw mat. Waking with a start, Bento greeted his friends without any great enthusiasm. He confessed to having developed a certain fondness for the house. After the whale, he would get some furniture, of the type that can be stood up against the wall. But his most ambitious plans were reserved for the carpets. Anything that was floor, or looked like it, would be carpeted. Even the immediate vicinity of the house too, because sand is annoying and seems to move together with ones feet. And there would be a special carpet which would extend along the sands, joining the house to the place where the self-same whale would disgorge.

Finally, one of his friends let the cat out of the bag.

'You know, Bento: back in Maputo it's being rumoured you're a reactionary. You're here like this because of this business of arms, or whatever they're called.'

'Arms?'

'Yes,' another visitor chipped in helpfully. *'You know that South Africa is supplying the bandits. They receive arms which come by way of the sea. That's why they're talking a lot about you.'*

He began to fret. *'Hey, boys, I can't sit still any more. I don't know who's receiving these arms,'* he kept repeating. *'I'm waiting for the whale, that's all.'*

They argued. Bento remained in the forefront of the discussion. Who could be certain that the whale didn't come from the socialist countries? Even the schoolmaster, Senhor Agostinho, whom they all knew, had said that all he needed now was to see pigs fly.

'Hold it there. Now you're starting on a story about pigs before anyone's even seen the stupid whale.'

Among the visitors there was one who belonged to the cadres and who said there was an explanation. That the whale and the pigs . . .

'Wait, the pigs have nothing to do with . . .'

'Okay, leave the pigs out of it, but the whale is an invention of the imperialists to stultify the people and make them always wait for food to arrive from abroad.'

'But are the imperialists making up this story of the whale?'

'They invented it, yes. This rumour . . .'

'But who gave eyes to the people who saw it? Was it the imperialists?'

'Okay, Bento, you can stay, but we're going now.'

And his friends left, convinced that there was sorcery at work there. Somebody had given Bento medicine to make him get lost in the sands of that idiotic expectation.

One night, with the sea roaring in endless anger, Bento awoke with a start. He was trembling as if suffering a bout of malaria. He felt his legs: they were burning. But there was some sign in the wind, some sense of foreboding emanating from the darkness, which obliged him to get up and go outside. Was it a promise? Or was it disaster? He went over to the door. The sand had come away from its resting place and seemed like a maddened whip. Suddenly, underneath the little whirlwind of sand, he saw the carpet, the same carpet he had laid in his dream. If it were true, if the carpet were there, then the whale had arrived. He tried to adjust his eyes as if to discharge his emotion, but giddiness overturned his vision, and his hands sought the doorpost for support. He set off through the sand, stark naked, tiny as a seagull with broken wings. He could not hear his own voice, he did not know whether it was he who was shouting. The voice came nearer and nearer. It exploded inside his head. Now he began to wade into the sea. He felt it cold, burning his tense nerves. Further ahead of him there was a dark patch which came and went like the throbbing heart of a hangover. It could only be that elusive whale.

As soon as he had unloaded the first items of merchandise, he would give himself something to eat because hunger had been vying for his body for a long time now. Only afterwards would he see to the rest, making use of the old crates in the house.

He thought about the work that remained to be done as he advanced through the water, which now came up to his waist. He felt lighthearted, as if anguish had drained his soul. A second voice addressed him, biting his last remaining senses. There is no whale, these waters are going to be your tomb, and punish you for the dream you nourished. But to die just like that for nothing? No, the creature was there, he could hear it breathing, that deep rumble was no longer the storm, but the whale calling for him. He was aware that he could hardly feel anything any more, just the coldness of the water lapping at his chest. What invention was this? Didn't I tell you that you needed to have faith, more faith than doubt?

The only inhabitant of the storm, Bento João Mussavele waded on into the sea, and into his dream.

When the storm had blown itself out, the blue waters of the lagoon subsided once again into the timeless tranquillity of before. The sands took their proper place once more. In an old abandoned house remained Bento João Mussavele's untidy heap of clothes, still warm from the heat of his final fever. Next to them was a satchel containing the relics of a dream. There were those who claimed that those clothes and that satchel were proof of the presence of an enemy who was responsible for receiving arms. And that these arms were probably transported by submarines which, in the tales passed on by word of mouth, had been converted into the whales of Quissico.

How Old Jossias Was Saved From
The Waters

1. *Recollection of the olden days*

The earth was conversing with August and old Jossias stood
still and listened. The months are all in one another's belly, he
thought. And he pictured the arrival of the days, their different
clothes and colours. He knew that rain was bound to come
soon, he anticipated the drops playing the marimba* on the
sand.

*'The water is going to go and read the ground. It's going to lick the
wounds of the earth, like some stray dog,'* the old man would say.

And he fell back into silence, his eyes raised to measure the
clouds as a precaution.

*'It looks as if it's just half the rain. It will surely fit comfortably on the
land.'*

While he made these prophecies, his eyes softened with
promises, a procession of green taking charge of his dreams.

'The corn will call me "sir".'

And he already imagined himself a powerful man, grinning
in foreglimpsed delight at his future abundance. He was
assailed by the memory of the great famine of twenty years
before. He began his surrender to sleep, now that his thoughts
had lain down in the shadow of that recollection.

He remembered it clearly: the rain-making rituals were

*A type of xylophone.

carried out in the headman's house. The prayers were words with no beyond: not one drop had been persuaded to fall. For three years the elders had persisted, conversing with the dead who control the rain's pleasure.

Early that morning they had killed the ox. The women had prepared the *ngovo*, or corn liquor.

In the cemetery the elders asked the dead permission for it to rain. After prayers they would give the dead some drink by pouring liquor onto the graves.

'I'll be the one to carry the pots of ngovo' Jossias offered.

They gave him the proud privilege of that delivery. Respectfully, he set out over the baking sand of the tracks. On the way, he took pity on his tired arms and stopped. The pots were heavy. The heat and thirst whispered bad advice to him, bewildering him with invitations.

He drank, closing his eyes to the voice of the liquor. He came back for more three times over. Predictably, the alcohol began to befog his reason. The pots smiled at him, warm and plump. *'They look like Armanda when she dances in that inviting way only she knows how,'* he murmured.

'You? You are stirring up my blood!'

He spoke slowly, rolling his words without his head entering that thought. Armanda's voice warned him of the punishment, restoring his sense of judgement. And he once again addressed the pots.

'Girls, you are ruining my life. Provoking me like this? You'd better fasten your capulanas* again. I must finish the task I was told to do.'*

He tried to get up but was too heavy. He drank only half: the rest he spilled down his chest. When he stopped to look, the liquor had all but disappeared. There was a mere trace left at the bottom of the pots. He fell into a panic: how would he explain it to the elders? How would he tell the village that the

*A dress worn by women, akin to a sarong.

64

ngovo had deviated from its purpose? He had to find a way of muzzling his mouth, of sealing off the trouble it had uncorked.

He came upon an abandoned well and climbed down into the darkness. At the bottom there was a trace of stagnant water, awaiting his ingenuity. If he added the foul smelling water to the corn beverage, the clay pots would once again be full. The dead would not notice the difference, for their palate has forgotten the tastier vices.

Like the miners, he thought, as he let himself down the walls of the old well. He was hanging on by his hands, his feet feeling for the bottom when, suddenly, the walls collapsed. They fell, and it was as if the entire sky were dissolving into sand and dust, and the weight of the world were compressing his chest. *'Mother, I shall stay here underneath the bottom of everything, no one will ever find me,'* sobbed Jossias.

And there he lay quite still, buried, sleeping in the suburbs of death, expelled from the light and the fresh air. Hours of time passed and he thought of the never more. The memory of Armanda came to his succour. He clung to the freshness of the recollection, that face was his ultimate faith.

And the others when they came looking for him? Would they guess him to be underground, burrowing the last dregs of his life away like a mole? Would they have the patience to peel the earth until they found him?

But even his hope no longer had a will to it. To be rescued, what for? Drinking sand, sinking in a well, bidding farewell to the world, all that was nothing compared to what would follow. None of them would excuse him for what he had done. Not even Armanda.

When he got out he would have to choose remoteness, to live in the far distance, to grow old without either name or history.

2. *All the blue of the floods*

What is this? Has God abandoned mankind? Doesn't he care about the earth's misfortune?

So much rain had fallen that even the wells were beginning to spit. Even toads and snakes had lost their homes. And the old man asked:

'Hardship, why don't you take a rest? When afterwards has passed you can come back again . . .'

But the way of death is ever full of woes. And it rained even more, the November afternoons got wetter, the pestle and the sleeping mat dripped water together in the yard.

The old man was sitting in the shadow of his groans, only his sighs dreamt. For the rest, it was resignation which conspired to rule him. Is it possible to die so much because of this?

But he had learnt to soak his soul in the balm of the bound-to-be. And he consoled himself:

'Mealie flour is bound to visit me, I know it.'

Gradually, rain water covered the whole area. The rivers clung strongly to the sky and no amount of witchcraft was able to get rid of that water. Maybe the sun, with its last residue of heat, would take away all that blue. But no, the sun slid down the zinc, without drinking almost anything. It passed overhead as diffidently as a stranger.

'The sun's mouth isn't big enough any more,' the old man lamented.

3. *The Rescue*

The water was rising, objects and creatures just had to swim for it. When everything round about was joined to the water like steam, there appeared a motor boat bringing two blacks and a white. It was the white who spoke. What he said was to do with things he had never heard before. What were these words about, after all? Before, they had always been stupid remarks

66

directed at his name, the language of the Portuguese firing insults at his family. Now was this language not like that of the bosses?

'*It must be a ploy to take me away from the* machamba*, *to separate me from my things.*'

Or maybe it wasn't like that. The men wanted him to climb into the boat, they had come to save him.

The old man scratched his head, moving his hand from back to front.

'*Go where, if beyond the water all there is is water? Don't you see God wants us turned into fish?*'

The blacks, from behind the white, repeated the same warning, those who didn't leave in the boat would die, that was for sure. The old man smiled, incredulous:

'*Save me, you say? Save me from what?*'

And the old man remembered the accident in the mines of John, fire spreading havoc through the galleries, devouring lives and bodies, yes, that was real dying. When the rescue workers arrived, he sat down like a lost child and cried. But the rescuers did not stop to help him, instead they went on, searching for other more valuable lives. Another miner pulled him by the arms and shouted to him:

'*Do you want to be firewood, man?*'

Firewood? Wood is firewood even before it burns. To be firewood, he realised, is to die all alone like that, without anyone to weep for us. His number would merely be crossed off the list of contract workers. But smoke entered him by way of sadness and his lungs bade him seek other pastures. If a man saves himself, it is because it is his life's desire. Others are only the fuel of that desire.

And that was how he had remained alive to this day.

They rescued Jossias twice. They saved him from death, but they did not save him from life. For the others, for those who

---

*Small plot of land for cultivation.

had helped him, there were rewards, their photos appeared in the newspaper. Nobody mentioned that he, Jossias Damião Jossene, continued the same as before, up alongside the breadline.

'*Saving someone should be a complete service,*' he had concluded. '*It's no good lifting someone up and then abandoning them without wanting to know the afterwards of it all. It's not enough to be alive. Take my word for it, living is more than that.*'

And so that is how Jossias had come to a conclusion on the matter of dying and not dying.

Now in this particular case, what was the point of moving, and where? Beyond, there is only more water, the place this boat came from is water too. It's not even a boat any more, but an island with a motor. If I have to die then I prefer that death which comes swimming right up to the door of my house. The earth under here already has my hands, my life is buried in this ground, all it needs now is my body, that's all.

The rescue team began to get impatient with the old man's ranting. '*What does the fellow want?*' asked the white. The others didn't bother to translate, but just laughed. The old man's mad, let's use force to bring him aboard. We haven't got time, there are others to pick up, the old man's out of his mind.

'*Let me stay, I can't die far from my life.*'

They pulled him along by his armpits, sat him in the rear of the boat and covered him with a blanket.

'*Haven't you got a family?*'

It was the white who spoke. Family? Maybe you people are my family now, you had to put up with the trouble of rescuing me. He felt like answering but he was trembling too much.

'*Ask him in your language if his family isn't somewhere round here in the vicinity.*'

They asked him. He took his time in answering, for he wanted to speak good Portuguese. He gripped the old blanket tightly and turned his eyes towards the sea which lay around them, as if trying to discover the things that it covered.

'It's not cold in the water. Why don't you leave me there?'

The others laughed. They placed another blanket round his shoulders and gave him a cup of hot tea. Through his skinny fingers which shakily clasped the aluminium cup, there rose a strange warmth which he was unable to explain. And he began to feel like staying in that boat for good. He wished that his journey would have no end, as if they were saving him from time rather than the waters, as if they had freed him not from death but from his terrible and solitary waiting.

With the eyes of a child, he stared at the darkness swallowing up the land, the evening covering everything with night.

The illusion of night is that it kills the weariness of men, he thought as he closed his eyes.

The Tale of The Two Who Returned From The Dead

It is a truth: the dead ought not to return, to cross the frontier of their world. They only come and disturb our sadness. We already know for sure: so and so has gone. We comfort widows, shed all our tears.

On the other hand, there are those dead who, having died, persist in coming back. This is what happened in that village which the waters had wrenched from the earth. The floods carried the village away, pulled up by its roots. Not even the scar of the place remained. Many were rescued. Luís Fernando and Aníbal Mucavel vanished. They perished beneath the waters, swept along by the river's furious current like a pair of fish. Their deaths had been taken for a certainty when, one afternoon, they turned up again.

The living asked them many questions. Then, alarmed, they called the militia. Raimundo appeared, he who carried his rifle as if it were a hoe. He was trembling with fear, and he could find no other words than:

'*Show me your papers.*'

'*You're mad, Raimundo. Put that gun down.*'

The militiaman gathered courage when he heard the dead men speak. He ordered them back.

'*Go back from where you came. It's no use trying anything: you'll be thrown out.*'

The conversation was not getting them anywhere. Estêvão, who was responsible for guard duties, arrived on the scene.

Luís and Aníbal were allowed in so that they might explain themselves to the authorities.

'You're no longer on our list. Where are you going to live?'

The two apparitions were offended by the manner of their welcome.

'We were swept away by the river. We ended up God knows where, and now you treat us like a couple of infiltrators?'

'Wait, we'll have to speak to the director of social affairs. He is the only one who can deal with your case.'

Aníbal became even more dejected. *'So we've become a case, have we?'* A person is not a divorce, a lawsuit. Nor was it that they had a problem: they just had their whole lives to sort out.

The official arrived on the scene. He was a tubby man, his belly inquisitive, peeping out of his tunic. They were complimented with the respect due to the dead. The official explained the difficulties and the extra burden they represented, as two dead people who had returned without warning.

'Look: they've sent us supplies. Clothes, blankets, sheets of zinc, a lot of things. But you two weren't included in the estimate.'

Aníbal became agitated when he heard they had been excluded:

'What do you mean not included? Do you strike people off just like that?'

'But you have died. I don't even know how you came to be here.'

'What do you mean died? Don't you believe we are alive?'

'Maybe, I'm not sure any more. But this business of being alive and not alive had best be discussed with the other comrades.'

So they went to the village hall. They explained their story but failed to prove their truth. A man dragged along like a fish only seeks air, he's not interested in anything else.

After some consultation the official concluded rapidly:

'It doesn't matter whether you are completely dead or not. If you're alive, it's worse still. It would have been better to take advantage of the water to die.'

The other, the one with the tunic that played tug-of-war with its own buttons, added:

'We can't go along to the administrative cadres of the district and tell them a couple of ghosts have turned up. They'll tell us we've got ourselves mixed up in obscurantism. We could even be punished.'

'That's true,' agreed the other. *'We did a political orientation course. You are souls, you're not the material reality that I and all the others with us in the new village are.'*

The fat one added emphatically:

'To feed you, we'd have to ask for an increase in our quota. How would we justify that? By telling them we'd got two souls to feed?'

And there the conversation ended.

Luís and Aníbal left the village hall, confused and baffled. Outside, a crowd had gathered to watch them. The two apparitions decided to look for Samuel, the teacher.

Samuel welcomed them to his house. He explained why they had not been included in the ration quotas.

'The officials here aren't like the ones in other villages. They divert supplies. First they distribute them to their own families. Sometimes, they even say there isn't enough to go round when in fact, their houses are brimming full.'

'Why don't you denounce them?'

Samuel shrugged his shoulders. He blew into the embers to give the fire new strength. Red petals of flame spread the scent of light through the little room.

'Listen, I'll tell you a secret. Someone did complain to their superiors. They say that this week a commission is coming to investigate the truth of such allegations. You should take the opportunity to explain your case to the commission.'

Samuel offered them a roof and food until the commission of inquiry arrived.

Aníbal sat his thoughts down at the rear of the house. He gazed long and hard at his feet and muttered, as if he were talking to them:

'My God, how unfair we are to our body. What part of it do we take

most for granted? *The feet, poor things, which drag themselves along to hold us up. It's they that bear both sadness and happiness. But as they are far from the eyes, we ignore our feet, as if they didn't belong to us.*

Just because we are above, we tread on our feet. That's how injustice begins in this world. Now in this case, those feet are myself and Luís, ignored, fallen amongst the dust of the river.'

There was less light than a shadow when Luís came over and asked him what he was muttering about. Aníbal told him about how he had discovered his feet.

'You'd do better to think of how we are going to show these folk that we are real people.'

'Do you know something? In the old days, the forest used to scare me, so empty of people. I thought I could only live with others around me. Now, it's the other way round. I want to go back to where the animals are. I miss not being anybody.'

'Do be quiet now. This is becoming like a conversation between spirits.'

The two stopped talking, fearful of their shaky condition. They began to fidget with things, to scrape their feet on the ground, as if trying to prove the substance of their bodies. Luís asked:

'Can it be true? Might it not be that we really are dead? Maybe they're right. Or perhaps we are being born again.'

'Who knows, brother? It could be any of these things. But what is not right is that you should be blamed, forgotten, struck off the list, rejected.'

It was the voice of Samuel, the teacher. He came over with some mangoes which he gave to the two candidates for life. They peeled the fruit, while the teacher continued to speak:

'It's not fair that they should forget that, whether you're alive or dead, you still belong to our village. After all, when we had to defend it against the bandits, didn't you take up arms?'

'That's true. I even got this scar from an enemy bullet. Here, look.'

Aníbal got to his feet in order to show the others proof of his suffering, a deep groove that death had carved in his back.

'Everyone knows that you deserve to be counted among the living. It's fear alone that causes them to keep quiet, to accept lies.'

Standing there like that, Aníbal clenched his fist as if to squeeze out his anger. Drops of the sweet-sad juice of the mango fell to the ground.

'Samuel, you know about life. Don't you think it would be better if we left, if we chose another place to live?'

'No, Aníbal. You must stay. You are bound to win in the end, I'm sure. After all, a man who leaves because he is beaten, no longer lives. He will find nowhere else to begin again.'

'And you, Samuel, are you one of those who doesn't believe we are alive?'

'Be quiet, Luís. Let Samuel here advise us.'

'These people who bedevil you are bound to fall. It is they who do not belong here, not you. Stay, my friends. Help us in our plight. We too are not being considered: we are alive but it is as if we had less life, it's as if we were only halves. We don't want that.'

Luís got up and peeped out into the darkness. He walked round in a circle, returning to the centre, and coming near to the teacher:

'Samuel, aren't you scared?'

'Scared? But these people must fall. Wasn't this why we fought, to get rid of such scum?'

'I'm not talking about that,' replied Luís. 'Aren't you scared that they will catch us here with you?'

'With you? But do you really exist? Surely, I can't be with people who don't exist.'

They laughed, got up and left through the two doors of the house. Aníbal, before taking his leave, said: 'Hey, Samuel! Long Live the Revolution!'

Three days later, the commission arrived. It was accompanied by a journalist who had become interested in the story of Luís and Aníbal. He had promised to investigate the affair. If the matter could not be resolved, he would expose the activities of the village officials in his newspaper.

The commission met for two days. Then the villagers were summoned to a general assembly. The room was packed out with people who had come to hear the verdict. The chairman of the commission announced its solemn conclusions:

'We have closely examined the situation of the two individuals who arrived in the village, and have reached the following formal decision, namely that comrades Luís Fernando and Aníbal Mucavel should be deemed members of the population in existence.'

Applause. The meeting seemed more relieved than happy. The speaker continued:

'But the two apparitions would be well advised not to leave the village, or life, or anywhere else again. We have shown clemency this time, but will not tolerate this behaviour next time.'

The meeting now applauded with real conviction.

Next day, Luís Fernando and Aníbal Mucavel began to see to the question of the documents that would prove they were alive.

The Girl With A Twisted Future

Joseldo Bastante, the village mechanic, used his ears to seek an answer to his life's problems. When a traveller passed by, when a car stopped, he would come near and capture conversations. It was in this way that he managed to hear of some prospects for his eldest daughter, Filomeninha. For one whole week, news kept coming from the city of a young man who was achieving great success twisting and turning his body like a snake. The lad had been engaged by an impresario to show off his skill at turning his rear into his front. He roamed the country and everyone ran to see him. And so the young man earned enough money to fill boxes, suitcases and cooking pots. All this thanks to his being able to fold and rotate his spine along with his nether regions. The contortionist was mentioned time and time again by lorry drivers and each one added a twist to the elastic talents of the boy. They even went as far as to tell how, in one show, he had tied himself up with his own body, as if it were a strap. The impresario had had to help untie the knot; if he hadn't, then the lad would have been belted up to this day.

Joseldo thought about his life, his twelve children. Where would he find a future to share among them? Twelve futures, where? And so he took the decision: Filomeninha would be a contortionist, displayed and advertised along the highways and byways of afar. He ordered his daughter:

'From this moment on, you're going to practise bending yourself, to get your head as far as the floor and vice-versa.'

77

The girl began her gymnastics. She progressed too slowly for her father. In order to hasten his preparations, Joseldo Bastante brought from the workshop one of those enormous petrol drums. At night he would tie his daughter to the drum so that her back and the curve of the recipient would cling to each other like a courting couple. In the morning, he would pour hot water over her before she had woken up properly:

'This water is for your bones to become soft, flexible.'

When they unbound her, the girl was bent over backwards, her blood flow irregular and her bones disjointed. She complained of pains and suffered from dizziness.

'You can't wish for riches without sacrifices,' was her father's reaction.

Filomeninha was crumpling up for all to see. She looked like a hook without any more use, an abandoned rag.

'Father, I can feel a lot of pain inside me. Let me sleep on the mat.'

'No, little daughter. When you are rich you will surely sleep even on a mattress. Here at home we shall all lie in comfort, each one on his own mattress. You'll see, we'll only wake up in the evening after the bats have stirred.'

Time passed, and Joseldo was still waiting for the impresario to pass through the town. At the garage, his ears were like antennae listening for news of the showman. In the newspapers, his eyes hunted for clues as to the whereabouts of his saviour. In vain. The impresario was amassing riches in some unknown location.

Meanwhile, Filomeninha was getting worse. She was almost unable to walk. She began to suffer from bouts of vomiting. She seemed to want to cast her body out through her mouth. Her father warned her not to succumb to such weaknesses:

'If the impresario turns up he mustn't find you in this state. You're supposed to be a contortionist and not a vomitist.'

The weeks went by, heightened by Joseldo Bastante's anguish. In such a small place, what happens is whatever passes through. An event is never native. It always comes from

outside, it shakes souls, inflames time and then beats a retreat.
It goes away so quickly that it doesn't even leave embers with
which the residents might rekindle the fire if they so wished.
The world possesses places where its timeless rotation stops
and rests. This was such a place.

Time went filling up with nothingness until one evening
Joseldo heard from a lorry driver news of the appearance of his
lucky star: the impresario was in the city preparing a show.

The mechanic left his work and rushed home. He told his
wife:

'Make Filomeninha put on a new dress!'

His wife replied, puzzled:

'But the girl hasn't got a new dress.'

'I'm thinking of your new dress. Yours, woman.'

They stood the girl on her feet and clothed her in her
mother's dress. It was big and long, and it was obvious that
their sizes were not the same.

*'Take off your scarf. Artists don't cover their heads. Wife, put her hair
in plaits while I go and get the money for the train fare.'*

'Where are you going to get the money from?'

'That's none of your business.'

'Joseldo?'

'Don't keep on at me, woman.'

◇

Some hours later they left for the city. On the train, the
mechanic gloated over his thoughts: a fruit is not harvested in a
hurry. It takes its time, between passing from sour-green to
ripe-sweet. If he had looked for an answer, as others wanted, he
would have lost this opportunity. To those in a hurry he replied
proudly: to wait for is not the same as to sit around waiting.

Lulled by the rhythm of the carriages, Joseldo Bastante
continued to surrender his little daughter to the fate of the
stars, the fortune of those who are immortal. He looked at the

79

girl and saw that she was trembling. He asked her the matter. Filomeninha complained of the cold.

'*What cold? With all this heat, where's the cold?*'

And he searched for the cold as if temperature had a body which might come and touch him in the twinkle of an eye.

'*Don't worry, little girl. When we get some smoke in here, it will get warmer.*'

But the girl's shivers became ever more extreme, until they were even stronger than the rocking of the train. Nor did the oversize dress hide her shuddering. Her father took off his coat and placed it around Filomeninha's shoulders.

'*Now try and stop trembling or you'll make my coat burst its stitches.*'

They arrived in the city and began to look for the impresario's office. They walked down endless streets.

'*Hell, daughter, so many street corners! And all the same.*'

The mechanic dragged his daughter along, stumbling into her.

'*Filomeninha, stand up straight. They'll surely think I'm taking you to the hospital.*'

Finally, they came across the house. They went in and were told to wait in a small room. Filomeninha fell asleep in her chair, while her father entertained himself with dreams of wealth.

The impresario received them only at the end of the day. He did not beat about the bush.

'*I'm not interested.*'

'*But, sir . . .*'

'*There's no point in wasting my time. I don't want it. Contortionism is out, it's no longer a sensation.*'

'*It isn't? Just look at what my daughter can do with her head . . .*'

'*I've already told you, I'm not interested. This girl is sick, that's what she is.*'

'*This girl's what? This girl's got an iron constitution, or rather a rubber one. She's just tired from the journey, that's all.*'

'*The only thing I'm interested in now are guys with steel teeth. Those*' *sets of teeth you people sometimes have, strong enough to gnaw wood and chew nails.'*

Joseldo smiled humbly and said he was sorry that he couldn't be of service: *'I'm a mechanic, that's all. I use my hands to fiddle about with screws, not my teeth.'*

They left. The impresario remained sitting in his big chair, amused by that girl, so skinny inside her borrowed dress.

On the way back, Joseldo bemoaned his fate. Teeth, now it's teeth they want! Beside him, Filomeninha dragged herself along, shuffling her steps. They boarded the train and waited for it to pull out. Her father gradually became calmer. He appeared to be watching the bustle of the station, but his gaze did not reach beyond the murky glass of the window. Suddenly, his face lit up. Taking his daughter by the hand, he asked, without looking at her:

'It's true, Filomeninha: you have strong teeth! Isn't that what your mother says?'

And as he didn't get an answer, he shook the child's arm. It was then that Filomeninha's body fell, twisted and weightless, onto her father's lap.

Patanhoca, The Lovesick Snake Catcher

Patanhoca it was who killed the Chinawoman Mississe, owner
of the store in Muchatazina. Now as to the reason why he killed
her, I can't tell you that. People talk a lot, each one according to
his whim. When I asked, they gave me an answer. So I'm going
to tell you the story. Or rather, pieces of the story. Torn pieces
like our lives. We can join the bits but never complete the
picture.

Some say it was nobody who killed her. She died just like
that, from inside her body, on account of her blood. Others got
as far as to see the wounds through which the poison entered
the dead woman.

I don't want to present the truth, for I never knew it. If I
invent, then it's life that's to blame. After all, the truth is no
more than the mulatto daughter of a dishonest question.

I'll start with Mississe.

1. *The widow of distances*

Mississe was a widow, a Chinese one, a woman of secrets and
mysteries. Her shop was situated at the point where the roads
end and all that is left are the unpaved tracks of the poor. There
was no set time for opening and closing: her mood dictated this.
It was she who decided what time of day it was.

Happiness stepped out of her life and forgot to return.

Sadness was a closed padlock on Missise. They even said it was Chinese bewitchment and that her far off homeland, travelling in clouds of vapour, was tormenting her soul.

Nobody knew how she had come there, how she had abandoned her people. And China, as everyone knows, is a distance away. The journey is such slowness that a man has time to change colour. Her neighbours and customers wondered to themselves about her dead husband. And at night, whom did Missise share the cold with? Who was it who snuffed out her darkness?

When she had arrived in Muchatazina, she was still young. Pretty, say those who knew her then. The Portuguese came to visit her beauty on the sly. They failed to enter her favour, remained substitutes of nobody. The widow wrapped herself in a cloak of sourness, becoming ever more widowed. The Portuguese, rich ones even, would come out of there with heads bowed. They would pause in the garden, taking advantage of the shade of the many cashew trees. To distract their frustration they would tear the fruit from the branches. The cashew is the blood of the sun suspended, its fiery sweetness the juice we drink. Then they would walk away, venting their threats.

On Saturdays the widow would indulge herself in bazookas, large bottles of beer, first one, then another, and then more and more. She would finish when the beer had wetted all her blood.

The store gave off brightness, the generator chugging away to push out that light. Fumes and mysteries would seep from the window, the Chinawoman's incense drugging the moons. It was at such times that the pain of this woman could be heard. Screams echoed in the corridors, her voice spiralled down a dark well. One night they distinguished words in her wailing: *'My children! Give me back my children, murderer.'*

So there were children after all? How could that be if no one knew of them? The neighbours listened in astonishment to her lament. The widow groaned, screamed, howled. They tried to go to her asssistance, to wipe away her furies, but no one could get near. Shadow was ever present. Death was the only garden round her house, enclosing her widow's despair.

2. *Patanhoca, the snake mechanic*

Patanhoca was a sad figure, robbed of life's good fortune. Something had torn his lips away, leaving his mouth with no above and no below. His teeth never unclenched. His mouth, because of the way it never blinked, was like a hyena's envy. Can a living creature keep his whole soul behind his teeth? Certainly this was Patanhoca's punishment. It was said he was the devil who had come to Muchatazina. This was a lie. Who said what the devil's face looked like? Is it ugly? On the contrary, the devil is as beautiful as can be, so as to deceive us into choosing backwards. A man like that is not tempted by women: he loves snakes, crawling animals and things which don't demand beauty. The snake catcher had taught himself to be a bachelor.

Morning, evening and other times too, Patanhoca would shut himself away with his snakes. A snake mechanic, he would scrape the rust off their scales, and nurture their poisons. His was the art of those who have lost the skill of living, the devil's lore. It wasn't even worth looking for the truth behind his life's condition. Did Patanhoca really know the secret of snakes? The answer has no document or testimony. But the doubters, if in fact there were any, were never heard.

When the evenings began to disperse the daylight, that was when he would go out, when darkness cradled the oil lamp. The paths were already pitch black but Patanhoca would set his steps in the direction of the store.

When he arrived at his destination he put out the lamp and began the task of spreading his sorcery. His perch was there in her yard, he, an owl drawn towards the lights of Mississe. What was Patanhoca's motive for always spending the night there? Were his lingerings just distraction? There was a reason, and that was love.

Shame manacled the snake catcher's passions. Looking was the only reward reaped from the shadows and the silences. To reveal the heart without showing the body, to dispense help and kindnesses: that is what João Patanhoca had decided to do in the secrecy of his life. Isn't a widow more alone than anyone else? Where is the arm to defend her?

That arm was Patanhoca. His powers kept thieves away from the store. Every night, so they say, he would set his snakes free around the house. So many of these snakes were there that the sand was poisoned under the blanket of night. You didn't need to be bitten. It was enough for somebody to step into the yard. In the morning, no one could enter or leave before the snake owner's prayers had given the go-ahead. His words swept the yard clean and abolished the frontier. All this, all this guard work, Patanhoca did without asking for anything in return. He would rivet his eyes on the widow, but they were no longer eyes. They were the servants of Chinese whimsies.

3. *First night: the invitation*

Then one night the widow opened the door. Was she naked? Or was it a play of light which eliminated her clothes? She waved to him. Patanhoca stayed where he was without revealing himself. Then she beckoned him. Her voice was a mother's:

'Come out of the dark, come in!'

He did not move, guardian of fears, unschooled in matters of happiness. He had never had any. She called him again, this time more hoarsely. She went down the steps, and pushed forward into the darkness. She tasted the smell of the mixtures and potions spreading their terror. She had never set eyes on such a smell before.

86

'Get back inside Missise!'

This was Patanhoca's order. It was the first time he had spoken. The words came out spitting and scraping, without the shape lips could provide. The crickets fell silent, the night air stifled. The widow pretended she hadn't heard and went on without turning. Again Patanhoca shouted his warning:

'Be careful! Snakes!'

Then she stopped. He came nearer, keeping to the dark side. He held out a little cloth pouch:

'Warm up this tea: it's your medicine.'

'No, I don't need it.'

'What do you mean you don't need it?'

'All I want is for you to come and stay here.'

'Stay where?'

'To live here, together with me. Stay, João.'

He shuddered: João? His eyes closed, pained: can a word, such a trifle, do so much harm to a man?

'Don't say that name again, Missise.'

She advanced further, wanting ever more strongly to lean against his shadow.

'João? It's your name. Why can't I say it?'

Silence gave the crickets their leave. Men and animals speak in turn, such is the law of nature.

Can a man weep? Yes, if you awaken the child he has inside him. Patanhoca wept, but he couldn't shed tears, for he had no lips.

'Why don't you come back again?'

'I'm Patanhoca, snake catcher. It's not just a name I was given. I've got a snout, not the face of a person.'

'No, you're João. You're my João.'

He explained his sorrows, said his life was shattered and that when you want to pick up the pieces, it's always too late. The Chinawoman wearied of his lament:

'Then let me out. Release me from this nightly prison, these terrors, these snakes encircling my life.'

In his fury he threw the little pouch to the ground and moved away from the circle of light to which he had brought his sadness.

4. *Second night: the revelation*

The next night, Patanhoca returned earlier. She was already seated on the steps, like a queen, smothered in perfumes. Her bangles robbed her of age, and made her skin glow. Patanhoca forgot to cover his shame in the darkness, and approached the woman from the back. He called her but she didn't flinch.

'*Mississe?*'

The widow looked up and he shuddered. There before him were her twenty years, there was the prize sought by all the hunters of desires.

'*Mississe, you're chancing your luck. The snakes will bite you.*'

She moved up one step and invited him:

'*Sit here, João. Let's talk.*'

Back he stepped.

'*No. Speak from there, I'm listening.*'

'*João, come nearer. I promise I shan't look at you. I'll speak to your back.*'

He accepted. He remained coiled in his body.

'*Well then?*'

'*There is no other man, nor will there be. Just you, you alone.*'

'*Why did you ruin my life, Mississe?*'

'*Let's not talk about that problem, please.*'

'*We must talk.*'

She paused. The memory pained her, and it wasn't saliva she felt in her mouth any more – it was blood pushing out her words.

'*You killed them, João.*'

'*That's a lie, it was the snakes.*'

Her nerves started to play on her, and her mouth stumbled in anger:

'*And who brought the snakes? Wasn't it you? I warned you, I begged you so many times: take them away from here, make them vanish into thin air. But you always answered that you were an artist. An artist of what?*'

'*I was, I am. It was just on that night I was drunk. My secrets fled me, that's what happened.*'

She cried, didn't even hide her face. The moon wreathed her tears. Pearls were born. The warmth of the real ones faded with envy. Clumsily, he tried to put right past insults.

'*And who were they? Children without any future. Mulatto-Chinese, a race without a race. People make children in order to better them . . .*'

'*Be quiet, Patanhoca!*'

She raised both her body and her voice, the two suddenly mingled in one. She ran inside and slammed the door, sobbing.

Patanhoca, standing, his hands together on his chest, apologised without effect. Mississe's accusing voice reached him:

'*Everyone thinks you're good, but that's not true. They think you help me, with your snakes all around my night. I know, only I know the snakes are to hem me in. You want to imprison me for ever, so that I won't run off with other men.*'

He retreated slowly, hurting himself on her words. But that pain was almost good to feel and, from time to time, he dwelt on what she said.

'*You are evil, Patanhoca. It wasn't you who chose the snakes, but they who chose you.*'

He gave up and moved away, his soul reeling within. Jealousy of others, jealousy of the living, that was his wickedness. The others, whether they were handsome or ugly, could trade with each other by day. Only he didn't have the right currency. The others smoked, kissed, whistled, had a right to be greeted and bidden good day. Only he had nobody to grow tired of. That Chinawoman Mississe had stolen the fire which we can kindle in others.

5. *Third night: the counsel of sleep*

It was night, the last but one, and Patanhoca was still in his house. He lay on his mat ordering his thoughts:

'It's true. I killed those two little children, but I didn't mean to. That night, drink confused my hands. I swapped the medicines round. But that Chinawoman got her own back on me.'

And he closed his eyes as if that crippling memory hurt him, she giving vent to her furies upon his head, smashing the bottle, cramming his flesh with glass. Blood and beer flowed in one and the same froth, her screams passed out on the ground where he was made night. Everybody thought he had died. Even she did, she who had left him, his wounds and his glass, to the night mist. She moved to a suburb of the city and opened her business.

He had crawled through the darkness, hands and voices protecting his thread of life and leading him along paths that he alone knew. He tried to forget the Chinawoman but he couldn't. He launched the boat of his life in other waters: the same current took hold of it.

He decided to move to her area, he trapped himself as if the hunter of his own destiny. He found her and saw that he had not yet been replaced. Mississe showed her suitors the street, even those who were rich and powerful. Could it be that she was waiting for him?

Fear and shame inhibited him from revealing himself. He appeared through his snakes, sent to dispel the threat of thieves. Whether she took her time to understand, Patanhoca never found out. She did not display any change, but continued, a widow without expectations. Did her calmness belie her?

Such were the questions the snake catcher of Muchatazina, João Patanhoca, pondered on, as he laid his tiredness to rest. He fell asleep awaiting the counsel of dreams. He listened with attention to his visions. They told him the following: she had repented, forgiven him. He would be taken back, once again João, once again a name and a face. Once again loved.

6. *The last night*

Mississe had once more caused his heart to rejoice. She stood there in the cascade of light, extinguishing the stars. She alone glowed, her white blouse and skirt, her tousled hair dripping onto her shoulders. Patanhoca overflowed from his body: then it was true what the dream had said! She was prettifying herself to celebrate his return.

'Tonight, João, let's have fun.'

He made no reply, he was afraid he might snarl and shame the João she was calling. With a movement of the head, she beckoned him towards the corridor:

'Come in, João, let's drink.'

He climbed up the stone steps, shook the dust off his feet at the entrance, walked across the carpets, excusing himself at every turn. On a cupboard in the living room, a large photograph of their happiness was exhibited, a picture of them both and their two children commemorating life together.

He seated himself awkwardly. She served the glasses. It wasn't beer, but one of those wines that make you feel dizzy before you even drink it. He unravelled memories, sweet trifles flowed between them, from one glass to another. He began to lose his inhibitions and drink dribbled shamelessly down his chin.

'I'm going to stop drinking, Mississe. I'm seeing the world go by at high speed.'

She wore a strange smile, which was too placid.

'No, João. Drink your fill. I want you to drink. Afterwards, I have a request.' And adversary of empty glasses, she filled another one. João was puzzled by the request, worried by that afterwards

she promised. Hopes and fears crossed within him and he said what he didn't want, ever wanting what he did not say.

'*Missise: it wasn't the medicines that I swapped round. It was myself I swapped. Now, am I João or Patanhoca?*'

She took his hands, made them one and spoke:

'*João, please, listen: go to your house and bring me that medicine you know about. I want to take it tonight.*'

So this was the request? Or maybe it was a trap, hopes tricking him.

'*I can't woman. I'm pissed; I have no legs to find my way with.*'

'*Go, João. You know the way with your eyes closed.*'

He looked around him: the linen tablecloth, the photograph, things from times that had fled them, they were there, silent witnesses to their disjoined lives. Missise persisted. She got up and leaned her hot flavoured body against him, placing her hands on Patanhoca's sweating back. He felt uneasy, unable to take any more.

He got up abruptly, turned towards the corridor and went. He found it difficult to keep to the line of his route. At the end, almost repentant, he turned round:

'*But listen here: what medicine is it, Missise? The snake vaccine?*'

She didn't answer, remained with her back to him, clearing away the plates and glasses.

'*Do you know, Missise? The only remedy, do you know what it is?*'

And he laughed, snorting loudly. She looked at him, saddened. How hard it was to look at that laugh he wore, but which didn't belong to him.

'*Missise, I'm telling you: the proper medicine is that wine we've just finished.*'

'*It's late. Hurry up João.*'

He struggled down the steps and walked off into the night. She still seemed to say something he didn't understand; he shook his head, confused. Could it be that he had heard her correctly? Going back to China, was that what she had said? I yearn for the land about to be born? Ravings of a Chinawoman, he concluded quietly.

He smiled sympathetically. The old woman must be drunk, poor thing, she even deserved it. This is what João Patanhoca thought as he stumbled along the path. He felt pity for her. After all, she was the widow of a man who was still alive, he himself. And so many years had passed since she had last taken her lace blouse from the cupboard, so many years since she had spread the white tablecloth on her table for visitors.

The Ex-future Priest and His Would-be Widow

Life is a web weaving a spider. Whether the creature believes himself a hunter in his own home or not, it matters little. The instant turns round and he becomes the quarry in an intruder's trap. This will be proved in the following tale which occurred in real though humble surroundings.

It concerned Benjamim. Ever since he was little, he had been a devotee of absences, he had lived parallel to heaven. Others played, celebrating the insignificant nothings of childhood. Only Benjamim withered among the Scriptures, amid saints and incense. Even his parents, who wished him sober and orderly, thought it too much.

'Go and play, Ben. Take advantage of your years.'

But Ben, unhearing, went on shedding his boyhood. His body matured into an age beyond his own. Nights filed by, bent themselves concave for the benefit of boys and girls. Only our friend's hands remained joined, stuck together, immaculate. Benjamim lived a life more lofty than the souls.

Until one day Anabela appeared, Anabelissima. She was pure candy, capable of publishing desires in the most prudish of eyes. Anabela fell for Benjamim. The poor man didn't even react to her: with a hedgehog's skill he rolled himself into an ever tighter ball. The girl sent him love notes, messages more sighed than scribbled. Anabela unwrapped herself before his eyes. But it's always like that: when there's a chance in the air

95

there isn't the ware. And for every forward woman a timid man. Let us T our crosses. Take each case on its merits.

The whole neighbourhood, meanwhile, entertained its thousand mouths with the tale of the romantic disencounter. In a nearby bar, people commented:

'Women? The more they wiggle their hips, the more they close their heart.'

'I know what it is she wants: cash, a fat wallet. But the only good thing that's free is rain.'

'No, it's not a matter of money. After all, think of Henrique, a mulatto just like her, he was turned down when he offered her the ring.'

There was only one truth though: Anabela, coveted by all, only had eyes for Benjamim. While he, taciturn, followed his vows. He wanted to enter the Seminary, to study padreology. While he waited, his only concerns were his devotions. Ben was ever devoteful.

Anabela's attacks became more persistent. It seemed that the more difficult her catch, the more keenly she pursued it. Who knows whether desire does not feed off impossibilities? Anabela began to visit him at unhidden hours. Many saw her leaving Benjamim's house, brazen, indiscreet. The girl seemed to be inviting scandal. Even when pronouncing his name, her voice slid along: *'Benjamim: Bendyoumee?'* People started murmuring. For how long would the lad hold out, the zealot fend off the zealous?

'He won't stand it. Is any man rust-proof?'

But appearances are more powerful than events. And surprise of surprises: Anabela's belly began to swell. Anabela, the self-same Anabela.

Her father, the esteemed Juvenal, then took preventive measures against his dishonour. After all, everybody knew what had happened. Juvenal was a much feared man. They awaited the consequences. A finger on the bell of Benjamim's front door announced the storm:

'Senhor Benjamim?'

'Yes? What do you want?'
'I want to know the date.'
'What date?'
'The date of the wedding.'
'Wedding? Whose wedding?'
'Yours, Senhor Benjamim. The date of your marriage to my daughter Anabela.'

The cassava began to grow sour. Ben became a stranger in his own home. A citizen struggling for survival, he managed to mumble a protest. But the other continued:

'You're a seminarist? So what? I know them well: they're the worst!'

Juvenal, a father-in-law on the eve of his making, was not about to accept argument and lies: the child in the womb was beyond doubt, legitimate and unconditional. And so the man went away, leaving Benjamim on the threshold of night. His thoughts were drained of memory, speechless. When all is said and done, no sadness can be explained, for it is a wound beyond the body, a pain on the far side of sentiment. And Benjamim's anguish was a flood covering everything. He imagined himself under the towel of darkness, as if life and death were symmetrical to him. All because of a mistake, his dream had been shattered. No longer was he to be a priest, his only ambition. And he would have to marry someone who only inspired anxiety in him. Deprived of earthly succour, Benjamim prayed. And he did so with such burning fervour that he wore through all his trousers at the knees. Even the ones from his wedding suit had to be sewn up.

Inevitably they were married. Anabela and Benjamim, and vice versa. Along with them, their families were joined in matrimony, names and destinies crossed paths. Their lives began to mingle with each other, and they became mutual witnesses of their intimacies. Their mornings to their nights

97

were full of misunderstanding. He, virginious, only kept his knee-caps busy, with his continual genuflexions. She ever yearning for night-long dances, and other distractivities.

And then in the end, her pregnancy was not consummated. Not that she had an abortion or miscarriage. Nothing like that. Anabela just disembellied mysteriously. Benjamim asked no questions: better to feign ignorance. And that's how it was.

Anabela meanwhile grew tired of parading her beauty without Ben exercising his masculine functions. So she decided to consult a neighbour, Bila by name, an elderly retired nurse.

'What's the matter, little neighbour?'

She replied that it was a very intimate problem, and the neighbour invited her in. Anabela, embarrassed, occupied a meagre edge of chair. She cast her eyes nervously round the room:

'I'm sorry, Senhor Bila. I haven't yet found a deaf wall.'

The nurse smiled benevolently, reassuring the girl. Let her speak freely: his were the most trustworthy of walls. Anabela confessed the reason for her unhappiness: the half-baked Benjamim. The old man listened to her words, her tears, her sighs. At the end, he summed it all up.

'You mean, he husbanded you but doesn't exercise sovereignty.'

She approved of his conclusion but did not agree with his next judgement:

'It's something that's plain to see, Anabela. I can see that you're not a complete wife. You always look a little downcast.'

She raised her hand, trying to interrupt, but Bila went on: *'Ben surprises me, so sturdy in his body'*. And then he laughed: *'He's like a sack of coal: he looks strong but can't stand up straight'*.

'It's not what you think, Senhor. I just want you to help poor Ben.'

'I'm sorry, Anabela, but it's not possible.'

He divulged his limitations: as a nurse he knew nothing, as a neighbour he could do less still.

'These things don't lie within the scope of hospitals.'

Bila got up. He pulled out a handkerchief and wiped his face.

Then, he went to the window and looked out at nothingness. He settled himself inside his coat before speaking.

'The cure for these ills can only be found in tradition. But you city people are already beginning to deny . . .'

'I don't deny anything. Ben would just never agree because of his religion.'

'But what do you mean? Is loving your own woman against any religion?'

'No, but this business of witchcraft . . .'

'Leave the matter with me, Anabela. I will persuade Ben; I have known him for a long time.'

The nurse explained the procedure: the stricken husband would begin by bathing in an infusion of roots.

'It is to wash away his bewitchment.'

Anabela was dubious, she wanted details. Bewitchment? Yes, for that was where her husband's misfortune stemmed from. The roots would wash poor Ben clean of his bewitchment. After that, Bila continued, he would be vaccinated.

'Then that's where you as a nurse come in, Senhor Bila.'

The neighbour shook his head. It was a traditional vaccine, made from the dusts of the fire, the ashes from the bone of a lion.

'A lion? Where can you find lions nowadays?'

'They're old lions, colonial ones. Guaranteed quality.'

The vaccine would be administered by an old witch he knew, capable of such arts as to be able to inflame an old anthill with passion. Even foreign aid workers went to consult her. The witch, according to the neighbour, had several international caps to her name. But Benjamim would have to move, with both luggage and soul, to the witch's residence.

'A training course, as some people might call it.'

The final test would be done with the old woman herself. If Benjamim had been properly cleansed, he would never again waste a chance with the lovely Anabela.

'Sleep with the old woman, my Benjamim?'

There was no alternative, said the nurse. Sores in the mouth are healed with saliva. She argued her fears:

'I've heard it said that there are men who only manage to do it with old women, those of very advanced age. With young women, they can't.'

Anabela went home full of doubts. A nightmare tormented her for many nights. She dreamt that on falling asleep she became an old woman, covered in wrinkles and scales. She aged at the precise moment that she fell into sleep. Her husband remained unaware of such changes from beauty to hideousness and vice versa. In one such dream however, after they had fulfilled their love, she fell asleep while he contemplated her with passion. Then, before his very eyes, the astonishing transformation took place. Her smooth skin crinkled, her fresh young body withered. He was startled, almost abandoned by the breath of life. He rushed next door to consult Bila.

'I need a medicine man to undo the spell cast over Anabela.'

Bila answered with a question: how did he know whether Anabela was not in fact an old woman who made herself young during the day?

'What difference does it make?'

'A lot, Ben, a lot. If your woman is the one you saw asleep, then you will be stuck with a wrinkled hag for the rest of your life.'

'But I want to undo the wizardry.'

'Very well. But afterwards don't say I didn't warn you.'

Still in the depths of the dream, Anabela awoke one misty morning. Looking at herself in the mirror, she saw that she was shrivelled up. She looked as if she had just died and then suddenly changed her mind. She shook the mirror until she saw her face shatter into splinters, but each piece of glass confirmed her manifold wrinkles. She washed herself in lukewarm water, and rubbed herself with herbal creams. To no effect. The wrinkles persisted, stubborn, invincible. And when she tried to leave the room, her torpid legs failed her.

Anabela would awaken from the nightmare, covered in

sweat. She would run to the mirror to check her appearance. The mirror reflected her, smooth and resplendent. She would sigh with relief, consoled by reality.

The bad dreams continued even after Benjamim's departure to the witch's house. Anabela could not imagine what arguments the nurse had used to convince her husband. But the truth is that Benjamim packed a small suitcase and set off without saying a word. He remained on his cure for three weeks. Anabela counted the days on the fingers of her despair. Would he come back normal? Or would he bring new habits from his intimacy with the old woman? He arrived at last. Anabela stood looking askance, without asking anything. Benjamim was pale, more overturned than returned. He sat down on the bed and stared at his wife for a long time. She was puzzled by his behaviour. What soul was there behind this man?

They sat there in silence for some time. Then Ben signalled her to come closer. Anabela got up, already feeling the volcano of her desires smouldering in her breast. She knelt before her husband:

'What is it, Ben?'

His arm wandered drunkenly in the vicinity of her bosom. She smiled and came nearer. Benjamim whispered something, it seemed more like a sigh than a word. The chill of an invisible hand caused the young wife to shiver.

'I want,' he said.

She began to unbutton herself, her dress appeared to tremble under her fingers. She came and sat next to him, waiting. Another whisper slipped past Benjamim's lips:

'I want . . .'

'So do I, my darling.'

'I want water. Give me some water, Anabela.'

A deep disappointment ran through her flesh. She sat still, between disbelief and frustration. In the midst of her delay, Benjamim suddenly got up. But before he could take a step, he had an attack of dizziness and collapsed on the floor with less substance than a mat.

They picked him up and lay him in bed; they tried in vain to wake him up. But Benjamim remained on the other side of his eyelids: his breathing was irregular. Anabela wept for her husband in that vegetable state, speaking to him tenderly as if he could still hear her. She spent sleepless nights, tending the creature who lay there beside her.

Time passed beyond lapse. One night, when the moon had already unfurled, Anabela fell asleep, vanquished by tiredness. In the depth of her slumber, however, she felt a shiver as if someone were touching her. She lay quite still, waiting. There was no doubt about it: they were hands practising the art of tenderness. Now they were enveloping her waist and filling her with a warmth which for so long had been wasted in sighs. Her heart began to beat faster: who could be the author of such desires? Benjamim? No, it couldn't be him if he had never dared, even before the accident. So she pretended to sleep and her anonymous lover unfolded himself in the mirror of her body, sea and shore flowed into each other. With her eyes still shut, she received this intruder, this picklock of her unhappy solitude. The sightless encounter repeated itself night after night. With closed lids, she would welcome the stranger. They loved each other with fury but without speaking. She was scared that Benjamim might wake up and catch her unknown lover in the act. Night hour followed night hour replete with moans, and the deep sighs of those who are losing their very life.

Until one day, Bila the nurse, on his daily visit to the patient, announced:

'Benjamim has begun to twitch his fingers. Tomorrow he will wake up completely.'

There was cheering and laughter. Everyone rejoiced. Everyone except Anabela. Her indifferent expression was noticed by her in-laws. The mother, saving appearances, said:

102

'*Poor mite. She's so exhausted she can't even react.*'

The young wife had, in fact, taken on the grey countenance of a widow. And when she accompanied her visitors to the door, she could be seen to be holding back the onrush of tears. The nurse, anxious, called her aside.

'*What's wrong, Anabela? Don't you feel well?*'

She did not reply. She turned her face and the dyke of her intimate bitterness burst. She accepted a handkerchief and tidied her appearance. Then she pulled herself together, and said in a flickering voice:

'*Can't you leave him to sleep for a few more days? Only a few more days?*'

The nurse raised his head, surprised. She explained herself:

'*It's just that I wanted to be with him a bit longer. I wanted to so much, Senhor Bila.*'

'*With him? Who?*'

Once again tears fell. The neighbour, in embarrassed consent was less of a nurse, and more of a priest. Believing he had received the confession of an indiscretion, he set the young wife at ease:

'*Very well, my child. I understand perfectly: you're so pretty, so sought after. How could you keep yourself to yourself for so long?*'

And they both went to the room of him who lay on the verge of life. While the nurse prepared the syringes, she bent over her husband. Maybe he, the secluded and bashful Benjamim, was the only one who heard the secret she surrendered to him. Anyway, the nurse glimpsed something resembling a smile at the corner of Benjamim's mouth. And smiling too, he injected him with fresh depths of slumber.

The Barber's Most Famous Customer

Firipe Beruberu's barber's shop was situated under the great tree in the market at Maquinino. Its ceiling was the shade of the crab apple. Walls, there were none: which is why it blew all the cooler round the chair where Firipe sat his customers. A sign on the tree trunk displayed his prices. On it was written: '7$50 per head'. But with the rising cost of living, Firipe had amended the inscription to: '20$00 per headful'.

On the ageing timbers there hung a mirror, and next to it, a yellowing photo of Elvis Presley. On a crate, by the bench where the customers sat waiting, a radio shook to the rhythm of the *chimandjemandje**.

Firipe would weed heads while talking all the while. Barber's talk about this and that. But he didn't like his chitchat to tire his customers. When someone fell asleep in the chair, Beruberu would slap a tax on the final bill. Underneath the prices listed on his sign, he had even added: 'Headful plus sleep – extra 5 escudos'.

But in the generous shade of the crab apple tree there was no room for anger. The barber distributed affabilities, handshakes. Whoever let his ears wander in that direction heard only genial talk. When it came to advertising his services, Firipe never held back:

---

*A particular type of musical rhythm.

'I'm telling you: me, I'm the best barber there is. You can walk anywhere round here, look into every neighbourhood: they'll all tell you Firipe Beruberu is the greatest.'

Some customers just sat there patiently. But others provoked him, pretending to contradict him:

'That's fine salestalk, Master Firipe.'

'Salestalk? It's the truth! I've even cut top quality white man's hair.'

'What? Don't tell me you've ever had a white man in this barber's shop . . .'

'I didn't say a white had been here. I said I'd cut his hair. And I did, you take my word for it.'

'Explain yourself, Firipe, come on. If the white didn't come here, how did you cut him?'

'I was called to his house, that's what happened. I cut his, and his children's too. Because they were ashamed to sit down here in this seat. That's all.'

'I'm sorry, Master Firipe. But it can't have been a rich white. It must have been a chikaka*.'

Firipe made his scissors sing while, with his left hand, he pulled out his wallet.

'Ahh! You folk? You're always doubting and disbelieving. I'm going to prove it to you. Wait there, now where is the . . . ? Ah! Here it is.'

With a thousand cares he unwrapped a coloured postcard of Sidney Poitier.

'Look at this photo. Can you see this fellow? See how nice his hair is: it was cut here, with these very hands of mine. I scissored him without knowing what his importance was. I just saw that he spoke English.'

The customers cultivated their disbelief. Firipe replied:

'I'm telling you: this fellow brought his head all the way from over there in America to this barber's shop of mine . . .'

While he talked, he kept looking up into the tree. He was keeping a watchful eye in case he had to dodge falling fruit.

*A poor white.

106

'These bloody crab apples! They make a mess of my barber's shop. And then there are always kids round here, trying to get at them. If I catch one, I'll kick him to pieces.'

'What's this, Master Firipe? Don't you like children?'

'Like children? Why only the other day a kid brought a sling and aimed it at the filthy tree, hoping to shoot down an apple. The stone hit the leaves and, mbaaa! it fell on top of a customer's head. Result: instead of that customer having a haircut here, he had to have a head shave at the first aid post.'

Customers changed, the conversation remained the same. From out of Master Firipe's pocket, the old postcard of the American actor would appear in order to lend truth to his glories. But the most difficult to convince was Baba Afonso, a fat man with an impeccably groomed heart, who dragged his haunches along at a slow pace. Afonso had his doubts:

'That man was here? I'm sorry, Master Firipe. I don't believe a bit of it.'

The indignant barber stood there, arms akimbo:

'You don't believe it? But he sat right there in that chair where you're sitting.'

'But a rich man like that, and a foreigner to boot, would have gone to a white man's saloon. He wouldn't have sat down here, Master Firipe. Never.'

The barber feigned offence. He could not have his word doubted. Then he resorted to a desperate measure:

'You don't believe me? Then I'll bring you a witness. You'll see, wait there.'

And off he went, leaving his customers to wait with bated breath. Afonso was calmed down by the others.

'Baba Afonso, don't be angry. This argument, it's only a game, nothing more.'

'I don't like people who tell lies.'

'But this one isn't even a lie. It's propaganda. Let's pretend we believe it and have done with it.'

'As far as I'm concerned, it's a lie', fat old Afonso kept saying.

107

'Okay, Baba. But it's a lie that doesn't harm anyone.'

The barber hadn't gone far. He had walked no more than a few steps to talk to an old man who was selling tobacco leaf. Then the two of them returned together, Firipe and the old man.

'This is old Jaimão.'

And turning to the tobacco seller, Firipe ordered:

'You tell them, Jaimão.'

The old man coughed up all his hoarseness before attesting.

'Yes. In truthfully I saw the man of the photo. It was cut the hair of him here. I am witness.'

And the customers showered him with questions.

'But did you get to listen to this foreigner? What language did he speak?'

'Shingrish.'

'And what money did he pay with?'

'With copper coin.'

'But which type, escudos?'

'No, it was money from outside.'

The barber gloated, self-satisfied, his chest puffed out. From time to time the old man breached the limit of their agreement and risked using his own initiative.

'Then, that man went in the market for to buy things.'

'What things?'

'Onion, orange, soap. He bought baccy leaf too.'

Baba Afonso leapt from his chair, pointing a chubby finger at him:

'Now I've caught you: a man like that wouldn't buy baccy leaf. You've made that up. That category of fellow would smoke filter cigarettes. Jaimão, you're just telling lies, nothing more.'

Jaimão was taken aback by this sudden attack. Fearful, he looked at the barber and tried one last line of argument:

'Ahh! It's not a lie. I remember even: it was a Saturday.'

Then there was laughter. For it wasn't a serious fight, their scruples were little more than playfulness.

Firipe pretended to be upset and advised the doubters to find another barber.

'Okay, there's no need to get angry, we believe you. We accept your witness.'

And even Baba Afonso gave in, prolonging the game:

'I expect that singer, Elvis Presley, was also here in Maquinino, having his hair cut . . .'

◇

But Firipe Beruberu did not work alone. Gaspar Vivito, a young cripple, helped him with the clearing up. He swept the sand with care, so as not to spread dust. He shook out the cloth covers far away.

Firipe Beruberu always told him to take care with the hair clippings.

'Bury them deep, Vivito. I don't want the n'uantché-cuta to play any tricks.'

He was referring to a little bird that steals people's hair to make its nest. Legend has it that once the owner's head has been raided, not a single whisker will ever grow on it again. Firipe blamed any decrease in his clientèle on Gaspar Vivito's carelessness.

Yet he could not expect much from his assistant. For he was completely crippled: his rubbery legs danced a never ending *marrabenta**. His tiny head tottered lamely on his shoulders. He slobbered over his words, slavered his vowels, and smeared his consonants with spittle. And he tripped and stumbled as he tried to shoo away the children who were collecting crab apples.

At the end of the afternoon, when there was only one customer left, Firipe told Vivito to tidy up. This was the hour when complaints were received. If Vivito could find no way of

---

*A Mozambican dance.

109

being like other folk, Firipe paid more attention to jokes than to barbering skills.

'*Excuse me, Master Firipe. My cousin Salomão told me to come and complain at the way his hair was cut.*'

'*How was it cut?*'

'*There's not a hair left, he's been completely plucked. His head is bald, it even shines like a mirror.*'

'*And wasn't it he who asked for it like that?*'

'*No. Now he's ashamed to go out. That's why he sent me to complain.*'

The barber took the complaint in good humour. He made his scissors click loudly as he spoke:

'*Listen, my friend: tell him to leave it as it is. A bald man saves on combs. And if I cut off too much, I won't charge.*'

He circled the chair this way and that, then stood back to admire his talent.

'*There you go, get off the chair, I've finished. But you'd better take a good look in the mirror, otherwise you might send your cousin to complain later.*'

The barber shook the towel, scattering hairs. Then the customer joined his protests to those of the plaintiff.

'*But Master Firipe, you've cut off almost everything in front. Have you seen where my forehead reaches to?*'

'*Ahh! I haven't touched your forehead. Talk to your father, or your mother, if you want to complain about the shape of your head. It's not my fault.*'

The malcontents joined forces, bemoaning their double baldness. It was an opportunity for the barber to philosophise on capillary misfortunes:

'*Do you know what makes a person go bald? It's using another man's hat. That's what makes a man lose his hair. I, for instance, I won't even wear a shirt if I'm not sure where it's come from. Much less trousers. Just think, my brother-in-law bought a pair of underpants second-hand . . .*'

'*But Master Firipe, I can't pay for this haircut.*'

'*You don't have to pay. And you, tell your cousin Salomão to pass this way tomorrow: I'll give him back his money. Money, money . . .*'

110

And that's how it was: a dissatisfied customer earned the right not to pay. Beruberu only charged for satisfaction. Standing from morning to nightfall, weariness began to burden his legs.

'*Hell, what a dog's life! Ever since morning: snip-snip-snip. I've had enough! Living's hard, Gaspar Vivito.*'

And the two of them would sit down. The barber in his chair, his assistant on the ground. It was Master Firipe's sundown, a time to meditate on his sadness.

'*Vivito, I'm worried that you may not be burying the hair properly. It looks as if the* n'uantché-cuta *is losing me customers.*'

The boy replied with choked sounds, he spoke a language that was his alone.

'*Shut up, Vivito. Go and see if we made much money.*'

Vivito shook the wooden box. From inside there was the jingle of some coins. Their faces lit up with a smile.

'*How well they sing! This shop of mine is going to grow, mark my words. In fact I'm even thinking of putting in a telephone here. Maybe later, I'll close it to the public. What do you think, Vivito? If we only take bookings. Are you listening, Vivito?*'

The assistant was watching his boss, who had got up. Firipe walked round his chair, talking all the while, enjoying imagined futures. Then, the barber looked at the cripple and it was as if his dream had had its wings shattered and had plummeted into the dark sand.

'*Vivito, you should be asking: but how will you close this place if it hasn't got a wall? That's what you should be saying, Gaspar Vivito.*' But it wasn't an accusation. His voice lay prostrated on the ground. Then he went over to Vivito and let his hand ripple over the boy's dangling head.

'*I can see that hair of yours needs cutting. But your head won't stand still, always moving this way and that, fiddle-de-dee, fiddle-de-daa.*'

With difficulty, Gaspar climbed up into the chair and put the cloth round his neck. Agitated, the boy pointed to the darkness round about.

'There's still some time for a scissorful or two. Now see if you can sit still, so that we can hurry.'

And so the two preened themselves under the great tree. All the shadows had died by that hour. Bats scratched the surface of the sky with their screeches. Yet it was at this very hour that Rosinha, the market girl passed by, on her way home. She appeared out of the gloom and the barber stood hesitant, totally enveloped in an anxious look.

'Did you see that woman, Vivito? Pretty, too pretty even. She usually goes by here at this hour. I sometimes wonder whether I don't linger here on purpose: dragging time until the moment she passes.'

Only then did Master Firipe admit his sadness to himself, and another Firipe emerged. But he didn't confide in anyone: as for the mute Vivito, could it be that he understood the barber's sorrow?

'It's true, Vivito, I'm tired of living alone. It's a long time since my wife left me. The bitch ran off with another. But it's this barber's profession too. A fellow's tied here, can't even go and take a look at what's happening at home, control the situation. And that's what happens.' By this time he was masking his rage. He diverted the human grief from himself and imposed it upon the creatures of the earth. He threw a stone up into the branches, trying to hit bats.

'Filthy animals! Can't they see this is my barber's shop? This place has got an owner; it's the property of master Firipe Beruberu.'

And the two of them chased imaginary enemies. In the end they stumbled into each other, without a heart to be angry. Then, exhausted, they let out a chuckle, as if forgiving the world its insult.

It happened one day. The barber's shop continued its sleepy service, and on that morning, just as on all the others, gentle banter flowed from one topic to another. Firipe was explaining the sign and its warning about the tax on sleeping.

'Only those who fall asleep in the chair have to pay. It often happens

with that fat one, Baba Afonso. I start putting the towel round him and he starts snoozing straightaway. Now me, I don't like that. I'm not anybody's wife to have to put heads to sleep. This is a proper barber's shop.'

At that point two strangers appeared. Only one of them entered the shade. He was a mulatto, nearly white in colour. Conversation died under the weight of fear. The mulatto went up to the barber and ordered him to show his papers.

'Why my papers? Am I, Firipe Beruberu, disbelieved?'

One of the customers came over to Firipe and whispered to him:

'Firipe, you'd better do as he says. This man's from the PIDE.'*

The barber bent over the wooden crate and took out his papers:

'Here are all my bits of plastic.'

The man examined his identity card. Then, he screwed it up and threw it on the ground.

'Hey, barber, there's something missing in this card.'

'Something missing, what do you mean? I've given you all my papers.'

'Where's the photograph of the foreigner?'

'The foreigner?'

'Yes, the foreigner you sheltered here in your barber's shop.'

Firipe was puzzled at first, then he smiled. He had realised what the fuss was about and prepared to explain:

'But officer, this business of the foreigner is a story I made up, a joke . . .'

The mulatto pushed him, silencing him suddenly.

'A joke, let's see about that. We know only too well there are subversives here from Tanzania, Zambia, wherever. Terrorists! It's probably one of those you put up here.'

'But put up, how? I don't put anyone up, I don't get mixed up in politics.'

*The political police during the Salazar dictatorship.

113

The policeman inspected the place, unhearing. He stopped in front of the sign and read it clumsily under his breath.

'*You don't put anyone up? Then explain what this here means: "Headful plus sleep – extra 5 escudos". Explain what this sleep means . . .*'

'*That's just because of some customers who fall asleep in the chair.*'

The policeman was already growing in his anger.

'*Give me the photo.*'

The barber took the postcard from his pocket. The policeman interrupted his movement, snatching the photo with such force that he tore it.

'*Did this one fall asleep in the chair too, did he?*'

'*But he was never here, I swear. Christ's honour. That's a photo of a film star. Haven't you ever seen him in films, the ones the Americans make?*'

'*Americans, did you say? Okay, that's it. He's probably a friend of the other one, the one called Mondlane who came from America. So this one came from there too, did he?*'

'*But this one didn't come from anywhere. It's all a lie, propaganda.*'

'*Propaganda? Then you must be the one in charge of propaganda in the organisation . . .*'

The policeman seized the barber by his overall and shook him until the buttons fell to the ground. Vivito tried to pick them up, but the mulatto gave him a kick.

'*Get back you son-of-a-bitch. We'll arrest the lot of you before we finish here.*'

The mulatto called the other policeman and whispered something in his ear. The other one walked back down the path and returned some minutes later, bringing with him old Jaimão.

'*We've already interrogated this old man. He's confirmed that you received the American in the photograph here.*'

Firipe, smiling feebly, almost had no strength left to explain.

'*There, you see officer? More confusion. It was me who paid Jaimão to testify to my lie. Jaimão is mixed up in it with me.*'

'That he is, to be sure.'

'Hey, Jaimão, admit it: wasn't it a trick we agreed on?'

The old wretch turned this way and that inside his tattered coat, baffled.

'Yes. In truthfully I saw the man of which. In that chair he was.'

The policeman pushed the old man and handcuffed him to the barber. He looked round with the eyes of a hungry vulture. He faced the small crowd which was silently witnessing the incident. He gave the chair a kick, smashed the mirror, tore up the poster. It was then that Vivito became involved and began shouting. The cripple clutched the mulatto's arm but soon lost his balance, and fell to his knees.

'And who's this? What language does he speak? Is he a foreigner too?'

'The boy's my assistant.'

'Assistant, is he? Then he'd better come along too. Okay, let's go! You, the old man and this dancing monkey, get moving. Walk in front of me.'

'But Vivito . . .'

'Shut up mister barber, the time for talking's finished. You'll see, in prison, you'll have a special barber to cut your and your little friends' hair.'

And before the helpless gaze of the whole market, Firipe Beruberu, wearing his immaculate overall, scissors and comb in the left-hand pocket, trod the sandy path of Maquinino for the last time. Behind him, with his ancient dignity, came old Jaimão. Following him lurched Vivito with a drunkard's step. Bringing up the rear of this cortège were the two policeman, proud of their catch. Then, the humdrum haggling over prices ceased, and the market sank into the deepest gloom.

The following week, two guards arrived. They tore out the barber's sign. But as they looked round, they were struck by surprise: nobody had touched anything. Instruments, towels, the radio and even the cash box were just as they had been left, waiting for the return of Firipe Beruberu, master of all the barbers in Maquinino.

The African and Caribbean Writers Series

The book you have been reading is part of Heinemann's long established series of African and Caribbean fiction.

Details of some of the other new titles available are given below, but for further information write to:
Heinemann International, Halley Court, Jordan Hill, Oxford OX2 8EJ

CHENJERAI HOVE

Bones

Winner of the 1989 Noma Award, *Bones* is a confident and convincing prose poem which hauntingly conveys the struggle of Zimbabwean peasants and their difficulties in rebuilding life, post-independence. It received wide praise in Zimbabwe where it was first published.

ISBN 0435–905–767

RESHARD GOOL

Cape Town Coolie

Set against the natural beauty and social squalor of Cape Town in 1947 – just before the arrival of 'official' apartheid in South Africa – this novel tells the story of lawyer Henry Naidoo's increasing political awareness. His activities expose him to a wide range of people and ideologies which ultimately lead to tragic consequences.

ISBN 0435–905–686

PAMELA MORDECAI
and BETTY WILSON (EDS)
Her True-True Name

Like the scattered islands themselves, these fragments from
31 women writers display both the range and variety of
Caribbean cultures and traditions, and their underlying
tenacity and cohesion.

ISBN 0435–989–065

STEWART BROWN (ED)
Caribbean New Wave
CONTEMPORARY SHORT STORIES

This anthology offers a taste of the energy, commitment and
talent of a whole new wave of Caribbean writing. The short
stories, written by both new and internationally acclaimed
figures, are grounded in the lived experience of the
contemporary Caribbean and offer an ideal forum for the
expression of modern concerns.

ISBN 0435–988–14X